LESSING, DORIS
THE FIFTH CHILD.   c1988.

The Fifth
Child

DORIS LESSING

The Fifth Child

1988

ALFRED A. KNOPF

NEW YORK

THIS IS A BORZOI BOOK
PUBLISHED BY ALFRED A. KNOPF, INC.

Copyright © 1988 by Doris Lessing
All rights reserved under International and Pan-American Copyright Conventions.
Published in the United States by Alfred A. Knopf, Inc., New York.
Distributed by Random House, Inc., New York.

Library of Congress Cataloging-in-Publication Data
Lessing, Doris May
The fifth child.
I. Title.
PR6023.E833F54   1988   823'.914   88-2680
ISBN 0-394-57105-3

Manufactured in the United States of America
First Edition

2-91   1500

The Fifth
Child

HARRIET AND DAVID met each other at an office party neither had particularly wanted to go to, and both knew at once that this was what they had been waiting for. Someone conservative, old-fashioned, not to say obsolescent; timid, hard to please: this is what other people called them, but there was no end to the unaffectionate adjectives they earned. They defended a stubbornly held view of themselves, which was that they were ordinary and in the right of it, should not be criticised for emotional fastidiousness, abstemiousness, just because these were unfashionable qualities.

At this famous office party, about two hundred people crammed into a long, ornate, and solemn room, for three hundred and thirty-four days of the year a boardroom. Three associated firms, all to do with putting up buildings, were having their end-of-year party. It was noisy. The pounding rhythm of a small band shook walls and floor. Most people were dancing, packed close because of lack of space, couples bobbing up and down or revolving in one spot as if they were on invisible turntables. The women were dressed up, dramatic, bizarre, full of colour: *Look at me! Look at me!* Some of the men demanded as much attention. Around the walls were pressed a few non-dancers, and among these were Harriet and David, standing by themselves, holding glasses—observers. Both had reflected that the faces of the dancers, women more than men, but men, too, could just as well have been distorted in screams and grimaces of pain as in enjoyment. There was a forced hecticity to the scene . . . but these thoughts, like so many others, they had not expected to share with anyone else.

From across the room—if one saw her at all among so many eye-demanding people—Harriet was a pastel blur. As in an Impressionist picture, or a trick photograph, she seemed a girl merged with her surroundings. She stood near a great vase of dried grasses and leaves and her dress was something flowery. The focussing eye then saw curly dark hair, which was unfashionable . . . blue eyes, soft but thoughtful . . . lips rather too firmly closed. In fact, all her features were strong and good, and she was solidly built. A healthy young woman, but perhaps more at home in a garden?

David had been standing just where he was for an hour drinking judiciously, his serious grey-blue eyes taking their time over this person, that couple, watching how people engaged and separated, ricochetting off each other. To Harriet he did not have the look of someone solidly planted: he seemed almost to hover, balancing on the balls of his feet. A slight young man—he looked younger than he was—he had a round, candid face and soft brown hair girls longed to run their fingers through, but then that contemplative gaze of his made itself felt and they desisted. He made them feel uncomfortable. Not Harriet. She knew his look of watchful apartness mirrored her own. She judged his humorous air to be an effort. He was making similar mental comments about her: she seemed to dislike these occasions as much as he did. Both had found out who the other was. Harriet was in the sales department of a firm that designed and supplied building materials; David was an architect.

So what was it about these two that made them freaks and oddballs? It was their attitude to sex! This was the sixties! David had had one long and difficult affair with a girl he was reluctantly in love with: she was what he did *not* want in a girl. They joked about the attraction between opposites. She joked that he thought of reforming her: "I do believe *you* imagine you are going to put the clock back, starting with me!" Since they had parted, unhappily enough, she had slept—so David reckoned—with everyone in Sissons Blend & Co. With the girls, too, he wouldn't be surprised. She was here tonight, in a scarlet dress with black lace, a witty travesty of a flamenco dress. From this concoction her head startlingly emerged. It was pure nineteen-twenties, for her black hair was sleeked down into a spike on her neck at the back, with two glossy black spikes over her ears, and a black lock on her forehead. She sent frantic waves and kisses to David from across the room where she circled with her partner, and he smiled matily back: no hard feelings. As for Harriet, she was a virgin. "A virgin *now*," her girl friends might shriek; "are you crazy?" She had not thought of herself as a virgin, if this meant a physiological condition to be defended, but rather as something like a present wrapped up in layers of deliciously pretty paper, to be given, with discretion, to the right person. Her own sisters laughed at her. The girls working in the office looked studiedly humorous when she insisted, "I am sorry, I don't like all this sleeping around, it's not for me." She knew she was discussed as an always interesting subject, and usually unkindly. With the same chilly contempt that good women of her grandmother's generation might have used, saying, "She is quite immoral you know," or, "She's no better than she ought to be," or, "She hasn't got a moral to her name"; then (her mother's generation), "She's man-mad," or, "She's a nympho"—so did the enlightened girls of now say to each other, "It must be something in her childhood that's made her like this. Poor thing."

And indeed she had sometimes felt herself unfortunate or deficient in some way, because the men with whom she went out for a meal or to the cinema would take her refusal as much as evidence of a pathological outlook as an ungenerous one. She had gone about with a girl friend, younger than the others, for a time, but then this one had become "like all the others," as Harriet despairingly defined her, defining herself as a misfit. She spent many evenings alone, and went home often at weekends to her mother. Who said, "Well, you're old-fashioned, that's all. And a lot of girls would like to be, if they got the chance."

These two eccentrics, Harriet and David, set off from their respective corners towards each other at the same moment: this was to be important to them as the famous office party became part of their story. "Yes, at exactly the same time . . ." They had to push past people already squeezed against walls; they held their glasses high above their heads to keep them out of the way of the dancers. And so they arrived together at last, smiling—but perhaps a trifle anxiously—and he took her hand and they squeezed their way out of this room into the next, which had the buffet and was as full of noisy people, and through that into a corridor, sparsely populated with embracing couples, and then pushed open the first door whose handle yielded to them. It was an office that had a desk and hard chairs, and, as well, a sofa. Silence . . . well, almost. They sighed. They set down their glasses. They sat facing each other, so they might look as much as they wished, and then began to talk. They talked as if talk were what had been denied to them both, as if they were starving for talk. And they went on sitting there, close, talking, until the noise began to lessen in the rooms across the corridor, and then they went quietly out and to his flat, which was near. There they lay on his bed holding hands and talked, and sometimes kissed, and then slept. Almost at once she moved into his flat, for she had been able to afford only a room in a big communal flat. They had already decided to marry in the spring. Why wait? They were made for each other.

Harriet was the oldest of three daughters. It was not until she
left home, at eighteen, that she knew how much she owed to
her childhood, for many of her friends had divorced parents,
led adventitious and haphazard lives, and tended to be, as it is
put, disturbed. Harriet was not disturbed, and had always known
what she wanted. She had done well enough at school, and
went to an arts college where she became a graphic designer,
which seemed an agreeable way of spending her time until she
married. The question whether to be, or not to be, a career
woman had never bothered her, though she was prepared to
discuss it: she did not like to appear more eccentric than she
had to be. Her mother was a contented woman who had everything she could reasonably want; so it appeared to her and to
her daughters. Harriet's parents had taken it for granted that
family life was the basis for a happy one.

David's background was a quite different matter. His parents
had divorced when he was seven. He joked, far too often, that
he had two sets of parents: he had been one of the children with
a room in two homes, and everybody considerate about psy-
chological problems. There had been no nastiness or spite, if
plenty of discomfort, even unhappiness—that is, for the children. His mother's second husband, David's other father, was
an academic, an historian, and there was a large shabby house
in Oxford. David liked this man, Frederick Burke, who was
kind, if remote, like his mother, who was kind and remote. His
room in this house had been his home—was, in his imagination,
his real home now, though soon, with Harriet, he would create
another, an extension and amplification of it. This home of his
was a large bedroom at the back of the house overlooking a
neglected garden; a shabby room, full of his boyhood, and rather
chilly, in the English manner. His real father married one of
his kind: she was a noisy, kind, competent woman, with the
cynical good humour of the rich. James Lovatt was a boat
builder, and when David did consent to visit, his place could

7

easily be a bunk on a yacht, or a room ("This is *your* room, David!") in a villa in the South of France or the West Indies. But he preferred his old room in Oxford. He had grown up with a fierce private demand on his future: for his own children it would all be different. He knew what he wanted, and the kind of woman he needed. If Harriet had seen her future in the old way, that a man would hand her the keys of her kingdom, and there she would find everything her nature demanded, and this as her birthright, which she had—at first unknowingly, but then very determinedly—been travelling towards, refusing all muddles and dramas, then he saw his future as something he must aim for and protect. His wife must be like him in this: that she knew where happiness lay and how to keep it. He was thirty when he met Harriet, and he had been working in the dogged disciplined manner of an ambitious man: but what he was working for was a home.

Not possible to find the kind of house they wanted, for the life they wanted, in London. Anyway, they were not sure London was what they needed—no, it wasn't, they would prefer a smallish town with an atmosphere of its own. Weekends were spent looking around towns within commuting distance of London, and they soon found a large Victorian house in an overgrown garden. Perfect! But for a young couple it was absurd, a three-storeyed house, with an attic, full of rooms, corridors, landings. . . . Full of space for children, in fact.

But they meant to have a lot of children. Both, somewhat defiantly, because of the enormity of their demands on the future, announced they "would not mind" a lot of children. "Even four, or five . . ." "Or six," said David. "Or six!" said Harriet, laughing to the point of tears from relief. They had laughed and rolled about the bed and kissed and were exuberant because this, the place where both had expected and even been prepared to accept rebuff or a compromise, had turned out to be no danger at all. But while Harriet could say to David, David to Harriet, "Six children at least," they could not say this to anyone else. Even with David's quite decent salary, and Harriet's, the mortgage of this house would be beyond them. But they would manage somehow. She would work for two years, commute with David daily to London, and then . . .

On the afternoon the house became theirs, they stood hand in hand in the little porch, birds singing all around them in the garden where boughs were still black and glistening with the chilly rain of early spring. They unlocked their front door, their hearts thudding with happiness, and stood in a very large room, facing capacious stairs. Some previous owner had seen a home as they did. Walls had been pulled down to make this a room that accommodated nearly all the ground floor. One half of it was a kitchen, marked off from the rest by no more than a low wall that would have books on it, the other half with plenty of space for settees, chairs, all the sprawl and comfort of a family room. They went gently, softly, hardly breathing, smiling and looking at each other and smiling even more because both had tears in their eyes—they went across the bare boards that soon would have rugs on them, and then slowly up the stairs where old-fashioned brass rods waited for a carpet. On the landing, they turned to marvel at the great room that would be the heart of their kingdom. They went on up. The first floor had one large bedroom—theirs; and opening off it a smallish room, which would be for each new baby. There were four other decent rooms on this floor. Up still generous but narrower stairs, and there were four more rooms whose windows, like the rooms below, showed trees, gardens, lawns—all the perspectives of pleasant suburbia. And above this floor was an enormous attic, just right for the children when they had got to the age for secret magical games.

They slowly descended the stairs, one flight, two, passing rooms, and rooms, which they were imagining full of children, relatives, guests, and came again into their bedroom. A large bed had been left in it. It had been specially made, that bed, for the couple they had bought the house from. To take it away, so said the agent, would have meant dismantling it, and anyway the owners of the bed were going to live abroad. There Harriet and David lay down side by side, and looked at their room. They were quiet, awed by what they were taking on. Shadows from a lilac tree, a wet sun behind it, seemed to be enticingly sketching on the expanses of the ceiling the years they would live in this house. They turned their heads towards the windows where the top of the old lilac showed its vigorous buds, soon to burst into flower. Then they looked at each other. Tears ran down their cheeks. They made love, there, on their bed. Harriet almost cried out, "No, stop! What are we doing?" For had they not decided to put off having children for two years? But she was overwhelmed by his purpose—yes, that was it, he was making love with a deliberate, concentrated intensity, looking into her eyes, that made her accept him, his taking possession of the future in her. She did not have contraceptives with her. (Both of course distrusted the Pill.) She was at the height of her fertility. But they made love, with this solemn deliberation. Once. Twice. Later, when the room was dark, they made love again.

"*Well,*" said Harriet, in a little voice, for she was frightened and determined not to show it, "Well, that's done it, I'm sure."

He laughed. A loud, reckless, unscrupulous laugh, quite unlike modest, humorous, judicious David. Now the room was quite dark, it looked vast, like a black cave that had no end. A branch scraped across a wall somewhere close. There was a smell of cold rainy earth and sex. David lay smiling to himself, and when he felt her look, he turned his head slightly and his smile included her. But on his terms; his eyes gleamed with thoughts she could not guess at. She felt she did not know him. . . . "David," she said quickly, to break the spell, but his arm tightened around her, and he gripped her upper arm with a hand she had not believed could be so strong, insistent. This grip said, Be quiet.

They lay there together while ordinariness slowly came back, and then they were able to turn to each other and kiss with small reassuring daytime kisses. They got up and dressed in the cold dark: the electricity wasn't on yet. Quietly they went down the stairs of their house where they had so thoroughly taken possession, and into their great family room, and let themselves out into the garden that was mysterious and hidden from them, not yet theirs.

"Well?" said Harriet humorously as they got into his car to return to London. "And how are we going to pay for it all if I am pregnant?"

Quite so: how were they? Harriet indeed became pregnant on that rainy evening in their bedroom. They had many bad moments, thinking of the slenderness of their resources, and of their own frailty. For at such times, when material support is not enough, it is as if we are being judged: Harriet and David seemed to themselves meagre and inadequate, with nothing to hold on to but stubborn beliefs other people had always judged as wrong-headed.

David had never taken money from his well-off father and stepmother, who had paid for his education, but that was all. (And for his sister Deborah's education; but she had preferred her father's way of life as he had preferred his mother's, and so they had not often met, and the differences between brother and sister seemed to him summed up in this—that she had chosen the life of the rich.) He did not now want to ask for money. His English parents—which was how he thought of his mother and her husband—had little money, being unambitious academics.

One afternoon, these four—David and Harriet, David's mother, Molly, with Frederick—stood in the family room by the stairs and surveyed the new kingdom. There was by now a very large table, which would easily accommodate fifteen or twenty people, at the kitchen end; there were a couple of vast sofas, and some commodious armchairs bought second-hand at a local auction. David and Harriet stood together, feeling themselves even more preposterously eccentric, and much too young, faced with these two elderly people who judged them. Molly and Frederick were large and untidy, with a great deal of grey hair, wearing comfortable clothes that complacently despised fashion. They looked like benevolent haystacks, but were *not* looking at each other in a way David knew well.

"All right, then," he said humorously, unable to bear the strain, "you can say it." And he put his arm around Harriet, who was pale and strained because of morning sickness and because she had spent a week scrubbing floors and washing windows.

"Are you going to run a hotel?" enquired Frederick reasonably, determined not to make a judgement.

"How many children are you intending to have?" asked Molly, with the short laugh that means there is no point in protesting.

"A lot," said David softly.

"Yes," said Harriet. "Yes." She did not realise, as David did, how annoyed these two parents were. Aiming, like all their kind, at an appearance of unconformity, they were in fact the essence of convention, and disliked any manifestation of the spirit of exaggeration, of excess. This house was that.

"Come on, we'll give you dinner, if there is a decent hotel," said David's mother.

Over that meal, other subjects were discussed until, over coffee, Molly observed, "You do realise that you are going to have to ask your father for help?"

David seemed to wince and suffer, but he had to face it: what mattered was the house and the life that would be lived in it. A life that—both parents knew because of his look of determined intention, which they judged full of the smugness of youth—was going to annul, absolve, cancel out all the deficiencies of their life, Molly's and Frederick's; and of James's and Jessica's life, too.

As they separated in the dark car-park of the hotel, Frederick said, "As far as I am concerned, you are both rather mad. Well, wrong-headed, then."

"Yes," said Molly. "You haven't really thought it out. Children . . . no one who hasn't had them knows what work they make."

Here David laughed, making a point—and an old one, which Molly recognised, and faced, with a conscious laugh. "You are not maternal," said David. "It's not your nature. But Harriet is."

"Very well," said Molly, "it's your life."

She telephoned James, her first husband, who was on a yacht near the Isle of Wight. This conversation ended with "I think you should come and see for yourself."

"Very well, I will," said he, agreeing as much to what had not been said as to what had: his difficulty in keeping up with his wife's unspoken languages was the main reason he had been pleased to leave her.

Soon after this conversation, David and Harriet again stood with David's parents—the other pair—in contemplation of the house. This time they were outside it. Jessica stood in the middle of a lawn still covered with the woody debris of the winter and a windy spring, and critically surveyed the house. To her it was gloomy and detestable, like England. She was the same age as Molly and looked twenty years younger, being lean and brown and seeming to glisten with sun oil even when her skin was without it. Her hair was yellow and short and shiny and her clothes bright. She dug the heels of her jade-green shoes in the lawn and looked at her husband, James.

He had already been over the house and now he said, as David had expected, "It's a good investment."

"Yes," said David.

"It's not overpriced. I suppose that's because it's too big for most people. I take it the surveyor's report was all right?"

"Yes," said David.

"In that case I shall assume responsibility for the mortgage. How long is it going to take to pay off?"

"Thirty years," said David.

"I'll be dead by then, I expect. Well, I didn't give you much in the way of a wedding present."

"You'll have to do the same by Deborah," said Jessica.

"We have already done much more for Deborah than for David," said James. "Anyway, we can afford it."

She laughed, and shrugged: it was mostly her money. This ease with money characterised their life together, which David had sampled and rejected fiercely, preferring the parsimony of the Oxford house—though he had never used that word aloud. Flashy and too easy, that was the life of the rich; but now he was going to be beholden to it.

"And how many kids are you planning, if one may ask?" enquired Jessica, looking like a parakeet perched on that damp lawn.

"A lot," said David.

"A lot," said Harriet.

"Rather you than me, then," said Jessica, and with that David's other parents left the garden, and then England, with relief.

Now entered on to this scene Dorothy, Harriet's mother. It occurred to neither Harriet nor David to think, or say, "Oh God, how awful, having one's mother around all the time," for if family life was what they had chosen, then it followed that Dorothy should come indefinitely to help Harriet, while insisting that she had a life of her own to which she must return. She was a widow, and this life of hers was mostly visiting her daughters. The family house was sold, and she had a small flat, not very nice, but she was not one to complain. When she had taken in the size and potential of the new house, she was more silent than usual for some days. She had not found it easy bringing up three girls. Her husband had been an industrial chemist, not badly paid, but there never had been much money. She knew the cost, in every way, of a family, even a small one.

She attempted some remarks on these lines one evening at supper. David, Harriet, Dorothy. David had just come home late: the train was delayed. Commuting was not going to be much fun, was going to be the worst of it, for everyone, but particularly of course David, for it would take nearly two hours twice a day to get to and from work. This would be one of his contributions to the dream.

The kitchen was already near what it ought to be: the great table, with heavy wooden chairs around it—only four now, but more stood in a row along the wall, waiting for guests and still unborn people. There was a big stove, an Aga, and an old-fashioned dresser with cups and mugs on hooks. Jugs were full of flowers from the garden where summer had revealed a plen-itude of roses and lilies. They were eating a traditional English pudding, made by Dorothy; outside, the autumn was establish-ing itself in flying leaves that sometimes hit the windowpanes with small thuds and bangs, and in the sound of a rising wind. But the curtains were drawn, warm thick flowered curtains.

"You know," said Dorothy, "I've been thinking about you two." David put down his spoon to listen as he would never have done for his unworldly mother, or his worldly father. "I don't believe you two ought to rush into everything—no, let me have my say. Harriet is only twenty-four—not twenty-five yet. You are only just thirty, David. You two go on as if you believe if you don't grab everything, then you'll lose it. Well, that's the impression I get, listening to you talk."

David and Harriet were listening: their eyes did meet, frowning, thoughtful. Dorothy, this large, wholesome, homely woman, with her decisive manner, her considered ways, was not to be ignored; they recognised what was due to her.

"I do feel that," said Harriet.

"Yes, girl, I know. You were talking yesterday of having another baby straight away. You'll regret it, in my view."

"Everything *could* very well be taken away," said David, stubborn. The enormity of this, something that came from his depths, as both women knew, was not lessened by the News, which was blasting from the radio. Bad news from everywhere: nothing to what the News would soon become, but threatening enough.

"Think about it," said Dorothy. "I wish you would. Sometimes you two scare me. I don't really know why."

Harriet said fiercely, "Perhaps we ought to have been born into another country. Do you realise that having six children, in another part of the world, it would be normal, nothing shocking about it—*they* aren't made to feel criminals."

"It's we who are abnormal, here in Europe," said David.

"I don't know about that," said Dorothy, as stubborn as either of them. "But if you were having six—or eight, or ten—no, I know what you are thinking, Harriet, I know you, don't I?— and if you were in another part of the world, like Egypt or India or somewhere, then half of them would die and they wouldn't be educated, either. You want things both ways. The aristocracy—yes, they can have children like rabbits, and expect to, but they have the money for it. And poor people can have children, and half of them die, and expect to. But people like us, in the middle, we have to be careful about the children we have so we can look after them. It seems to me you haven't thought it out . . . no, I'll go and make the coffee, you two go and sit down."

David and Harriet went through the wide gap in the wall that marked off the kitchen to the sofa in the living-room, where they sat holding hands, a slight, stubborn, rather perturbed young man, and an enormous, flushed, clumsily moving woman. Harriet was eight months pregnant, and it had not been an easy pregnancy. Nothing seriously wrong, but she had been sick a lot, slept badly from indigestion, and was disappointed with herself. They were wondering why it was that people always criticised them. Dorothy brought coffee, set it down, said, "I'll do the washing-up—no, you just sit there." And went back to the sink.

"But it *is* what I feel," said Harriet, distressed.

"Yes."

"We should have children while we can," said Harriet.

Dorothy said, from the sink, "At the beginning of the last war, people were saying it was irresponsible to have children, but we had them, didn't we?" She laughed.

"There you are, then," said David.

"And we kept them," said Dorothy.

"Well, here I am certainly," said Harriet.

The first baby, Luke, was born in the big bed attended mostly by the midwife, with Dr. Brett there, too. David and Dorothy held Harriet's hands. It goes without saying that the doctor had wanted Harriet in hospital. She had been adamant; was disapproved of—by him.

It was a windy cold night, just after Christmas. The room was warm and wonderful. David wept. Dorothy wept. Harriet laughed and wept. The midwife and the doctor had a little air of festivity and triumph. They all drank champagne, and poured some on little Luke's head. It was 1966.

Luke was an easy baby. He slept most peaceably in the little room off the big bedroom, and was contentedly breast-fed. Happiness! When David went off to catch his train to London in the mornings, Harriet was sitting up in bed feeding the baby, and drinking the tea David had brought her. When he bent to kiss her goodbye, and stroked Luke's head, it was with a fierce possessiveness that Harriet liked and understood, for it was not herself being possessed, or the baby, but happiness. Hers and his.

That Easter was the first of the family parties. Rooms had been adequately if sketchily furnished, and they were filled with Harriet's two sisters, Sarah and Angela, and their husbands and their children; with Dorothy, in her element; and briefly by Molly and Frederick, who allowed that they were enjoying themselves but family life on this scale was not for them.

Connoisseurs of the English scene will by now have realised that on that powerful, if nowhere registered, yardstick, the English class system, Harriet scaled rather lower than David. Within five seconds of any of the Lovatts or the Burkes meeting any of the Walkers, the fact had been noted but not commented on—verbally, at least. The Walkers were not surprised that Frederick and Molly said they would be there for only two days; nor that they changed their minds when James Lovatt appeared. Like many husbands and wives forced to separate by incompatibility, Molly and James enjoyed meeting when they knew they must shortly part. In fact, they all enjoyed themselves, agreeing that the house was made for it. Around the great family table, where so many chairs could be comfortably accommodated, people sat through long pleasant meals, or found their way there between meals to drink coffee and tea, and to talk. And laugh . . . Listening to the laughter, the voices, the talk, the sounds of children playing, Harriet and David in their bedroom, or perhaps descending from the landing, would reach for each other's hand, and smile, and breathe happiness. No one knew, not even Dorothy—certainly not Dorothy—that Harriet was pregnant again. Luke was three months old. They had not meant for Harriet to be pregnant—not for another year. But so it was. "There's something progenitive about this room, I swear it," said David, laughing. They felt agreeably guilty. They lay in their bed, listening to Luke make his baby noises next door, and decided not to say a word until after everyone had gone.

When Dorothy was told, she was again rather silent, and then said, "Well, you'll need me, won't you?"

They did. This pregnancy, like the other, was normal, but Harriet was uncomfortable and sick, and thought to herself that while she had not changed her mind at all about six (or eight or ten) children, she would be jolly sure there was a good interval between this one and the next.

For the rest of the year, Dorothy was pleasantly around the house, helped look after Luke and to make curtains for the rooms on the third floor.

That Christmas, Harriet was again enormous, in her eighth month, and she laughed at herself for her size and unwieldiness. The house was full. All the people who were here for Easter came again. It was acknowledged that Harriet and David had a gift for this kind of thing. A cousin of Harriet's with three children came, too, for she had heard of the wonderful Easter party that had gone on for a week. A colleague of David's came with his wife. This Christmas was ten days long, and one feast followed another. Luke was in his pram downstairs and everyone fussed over him, and the older children carried him around like a doll. Briefly, too, came David's sister Deborah, a cool attractive girl who could easily have been Jessica's daughter and not Molly's. She was not married, though she had had what she described as near misses. In general style she was so far removed from the people in the house, all basic British—as they defined themselves relative to her—that these differences became a running joke. She had always lived the life of the rich, had found the shabby high-mindedness of her mother's house irritating, hated people being crammed together, but conceded that she found this party interesting.

There were twelve adults and ten children. Neighbours, invited, did appear, but the sense of family togetherness was strong and excluded them. And Harriet and David exulted that they, their obstinacy, what everyone had criticised and laughed at, had succeeded in this miracle: they were able to unite all these so different people, and make them enjoy each other.

The second child, Helen, was born, like Luke, in the family bed, with all the same people there, and again champagne anointed the baby's head, and everyone wept. Luke was evicted from the baby's room into the next one down the corridor, and Helen took his place.

Though Harriet was tired—indeed, worn out—the Easter party took place. Dorothy was against it. "You are *tired*, girl," she said. "You are bone tired." Then, seeing Harriet's face: "Well, all right, but you aren't to do anything, mind."

The two sisters and Dorothy made themselves responsible for the shopping and the cooking, the hard work.

Downstairs among all the people—for the house was again full—were the two little creatures, Helen and Luke, all wispy fair hair and blue eyes and pink cheeks. Luke was staggering about, aided by everyone, and Helen was in her pram.

That summer—it was 1968—the house was full to the attic, nearly all family. The house was so convenient for London: people travelled up with David for the day and came back with him. There was good walking country twenty minutes' drive away.

People came and went, said they were coming for a couple of days and stayed a week. And how was all this paid for? Well, of course everyone contributed; and, of course, not enough, but people knew David's father was rich. Without that mortgage being paid for, none of this could have happened. Money was always tight. Economies were made: a vast hotel-size freezer bought second-hand was stocked with summer fruit and vegetables. Dorothy and Sarah and Angela bottled fruit and jam and chutneys. They baked bread and the whole house smelled of new bread. This was happiness, in the old style.

There was a cloud, though. Sarah and her husband, William,

were unhappily married, and quarrelled, and made up, but she was pregnant with her fourth, and a divorce was not possible.

Christmas, just as wonderful a festival, came and went. Then Easter . . . sometimes they all had to wonder where everybody was fitting themselves in.

The cloud on family happiness that was Sarah and William's discord disappeared, for it was absorbed in worse. Sarah's new baby was Down's syndrome, and there was no question of them separating. Dorothy remarked sometimes that it was a pity there wasn't two of her, Sarah needed her as much, and more, than Harriet. And indeed she did take off on visits to her Sarah, who was afflicted, while Harriet was not.

Jane was born in 1970, when Helen was two. Much too fast, scolded Dorothy, what was the hurry?

Helen moved into Luke's room, and Luke moved one room along. Jane made her contented noises in the baby's room, and the two little children came into the big family bed and cuddled and played games, or they visited Dorothy in her bed and played there.

Happiness. A happy family. The Lovatts were a happy family. It was what they had chosen and what they deserved. Often, when David and Harriet lay face to face, it seemed that doors in their breasts flew open, and what poured out was an intensity of relief, of thankfulness, that still astonished them both: patience for what seemed now such a very long time had not been easy, after all. It had been hard preserving their belief in themselves when the spirit of the times, the greedy and selfish sixties, had been so ready to condemn them, to isolate, to diminish their best selves. And look, they had been right to insist on guarding that stubborn individuality of theirs, which had chosen, and so obstinately, the best—this.

Outside this fortunate place, their family, beat and battered the storms of the world. The easy good times had utterly gone. David's firm had been struck, and he had not been given the promotion he expected; but others had lost their jobs and he was lucky. Sarah's husband was out of work. Sarah joked dolefully that she and William attracted all the ill luck in the clan.

Harriet said to David, privately, that she did not believe it was bad luck: Sarah and William's unhappiness, their quarrelling, had probably attracted the mongol child—yes, yes, of course she knew one shouldn't call them mongol. But the little girl did look a bit like Genghis Khan, didn't she? A baby Genghis Khan with her squashed little face and her slitty eyes? David disliked this trait of Harriet's, a fatalism that seemed so at odds with the rest of her. He said he thought this was silly hysterical thinking: Harriet sulked and they had to make up.

The little town they lived in had changed in the five years they had been here. Brutal incidents and crimes, once shocking everyone, were now commonplace. Gangs of youths hung around certain cafés and street-ends and owed respect to no one. The house next door had been burgled three times: the Lovatts' not yet, but then there were always people about. At the end of the road there was a telephone box that had been vandalised so often the authorities had given up: it stood unusable. These days, Harriet would not dream of walking at night by herself, but once it would not have occurred to her not to go anywhere she pleased at any time of the day or night. There was an ugly edge on events: more and more it seemed that two peoples lived in England, not one—enemies, hating each other, who could not hear what the other said. The young Lovatts made themselves read the papers, and watch the News on television, though their instinct was to do neither. At least they ought to know what went on outside their fortress, their kingdom, in which three precious children were nurtured, and where so many people came to immerse themselves in safety, comfort, kindness.

The fourth baby, Paul, was born in 1973, between a Christmas and an Easter. Harriet was not very well: her pregnancies had continued uncomfortable and full of minor problems—nothing serious, but she was tired.

The Easter festivities were the best ever: that year was the best of all their years, and, looking back afterwards, it seemed that the whole year was a celebration, renewed from a spring of loving hospitality whose guardians were Harriet and David, beginning at Christmas when Harriet was so very pregnant, everyone looking after her, sharing in the work of creating magnificent meals, involved with the coming baby . . . knowing that Easter was coming, then the long summer, then Christmas again. . . .

Easter went on for three weeks, all of the school holidays. The house was crammed. The three little children had their own rooms but moved in together when beds were needed. Which of course they adored. "Why not let them sleep together always?" Dorothy, the others would enquire. "A room each for such little tiddlers!"

"It's important," said David, fierce; "everyone should have a room."

The family exchanged glances as families do when stubbing toes on some snag in one of them: and Molly, who felt herself both appreciated but in some devious way criticised, too, said, "Everyone in the world! Everybody!" She had intended to sound humorous.

This scene was at breakfast—or, rather, mid-morning—in the family room, breakfast continuing indefinitely. All the adults were still around the table, fifteen of them. The children played among the sofas and chairs of the sitting-room area. Molly and Frederick sat side by side, as always, preserving their air of judging everything by the perspectives of Oxford, for which, here, they often got teased, but did not seem to mind, and were humorously on the defensive. David's father, James, had been written to again by Molly, who had said he must "fork out" more money, the young couple simply were not coping with

feeding Uncle Tom Cobbleigh and all. He had sent a generous
cheque and then had come himself. He sat opposite his former
wife and her husband, and as usual both kinds of people were
observed examining each other and marvelling that they could
ever have come together. He looked fitted out for some sporting
occasion: in fact, he was off skiing shortly, like Deborah, who
was here with her little air of an exotic bird that had alighted
in a strange place and was kept there by curiosity—she was not
going to admit to admiration. Dorothy was there, dispensing
tea and coffee. Angela sat with her husband; her three children
played with the others. Angela, efficient, brisk ("a coper," as
Dorothy said, the "thank God" being unspoken), allowed it to
be known that she felt the two other sisters took up all of Dorothy
and left her nothing. She was like a clever, pretty little fox.
Sarah, Sarah's husband, cousins, friends—the big house had
people tucked into every corner, even on the sofas down here.
The attic had long ago become a dormitory stacked with mat-
tresses and sleeping bags in which any number of children could
be bedded. As they sat here in the great warm comfortable room,
which had a fire burning of wood collected by everyone yesterday
from the woodland they had been walking in, the rooms above
resounded with voices, and with music. Some of the older
children were practising a song. This was a house—and this
defined it for everyone, admiring what they could not achieve
themselves—where television was not often watched.

Sarah's husband, William, was not at the table, but lounging
against the dividing wall; and the little distance expressed what
he felt his relation to the family was. He had left Sarah twice,
and come home again. It was evident to everyone this was a
process that would continue. He had got himself a job, a poor
one, in the building trade: the trouble was that he was distressed
by physical disability, and his new daughter, the Down's syndrome baby, appalled him. Yet he was very much married to

Sarah. They were a match: both tall, generously built, dark, like a pair of gypsies, always in colourful clothes. But the poor baby was in Sarah's arms, covered up so as not to upset everyone, and William was looking everywhere but at his wife.

He looked instead at Harriet, who sat nursing Paul, two months old, in the big chair that was hers because it was comfortable for this function. She looked exhausted. Jane had been awake in the night with her teeth, and had wanted Mummy, not Granny.

She had not been much changed by presenting the world with four human beings. She sat there at the head of the table, the collar of her blue shirt pushed to one side to show part of a blue-veined white breast, and Paul's energetically moving little head. Her lips were characteristically firmly set, and she was observing everything: a healthy, attractive young woman, full of life. But tired . . . the children came rushing from their play to demand her attention, and she was suddenly irritable, and snapped, "Why don't you go and play upstairs in the attic?" This was unlike her—again glances were exchanged among the adults, who took over the job of getting the children's noise out of her way. In the end, it was Angela who went with them.

Harriet was distressed because she had been bad-tempered. "I was up all night," she began, and William interrupted her, taking command—expressing what they all felt, and Harriet knew it; even if she knew why it had to be William, the delinquent husband and father.

"And now that's got to be it, sister-in-law Harriet," he announced, leaning forward from his wall, hand raised, like a band-leader. "How old are you? No, don't tell me, I know, and you've had four children in six years. . . ." Here he looked around to make sure they were all with him: they were, and Harriet could see it. She smiled ironically.

"A criminal," she said, "that's what I am."

25

"Give it a rest, Harriet. That's all we ask of you," he went on, sounding more and more facetious, histrionic—as was his way.

"The father of four children speaks," said Sarah, passionately cuddling her poor Amy, defying them to say aloud what they must be thinking: that she was going out of her way to support him, her unsatisfactory husband, in front of them all. He gave her a grateful look while his eyes avoided the pathetic bundle she protected.

"Yes, but at least we spread it out over ten years," he said.

"We are going to give it a rest," announced Harriet. She added, sounding defiant, "For at least three years."

Everyone exchanged looks: she thought them condemning.

"I told you so," said William. "These madmen are going to go on."

"These madmen certainly are," said David.

"I told you so," said Dorothy. "When Harriet's got an idea into her head, then you can save your breath."

"Just like her mother," said Sarah forlornly: this referred to Dorothy's decision that Harriet needed her more than Sarah did, the defective child notwithstanding. "You're much tougher than she is, Sarah," Dorothy had pronounced. "The trouble with Harriet is that her eyes have always been bigger than her stomach."

Dorothy was near Harriet, with little Jane, listless from the bad night, dozing in her arms. She sat erect, solid; her lips were set firm, her eyes missed nothing.

"Why not?" said Harriet. She smiled at her mother: "How could I do better?"

"They are going to have four more children," Dorothy said, appealing to the others.

"Good God," said James, admiring but awed. "Well, it's just as well I make so much money."

David did not like this: he flushed and would not look at anyone.

"Oh don't be like that, David," said Sarah, trying not to sound bitter: she needed money, badly, but it was David, who was in a good job, who got so much extra.

"You aren't really going to have four more children?" enquired Sarah, sighing—and they all knew she was saying, four more challenges to destiny. She gently put her hand over the sleeping Amy's head, covered in a shawl, holding it safe from the world.

"Yes, we are," said David.

"Yes, we certainly are," said Harriet. "This is what everyone wants, really, but we've been brainwashed out of it. People want to live like this, really."

"Happy families," said Molly critically: she was standing up for a life where domesticity was kept in its place, a background to what was important.

"We are the centre of this family," said David. "We are— Harriet and me. Not you, Mother."

"God forbid," said Molly, her large face, always highly coloured, even more flushed: she was annoyed.

"Oh all right," said her son. "It's never been your style."

"It's certainly never been mine," said James, "and I'm not going to apologise for it."

"But you've been a marvellous father, super," chirruped Deborah. "And Jessica's been a super mum."

Her real mother raised her ponderous brows.

"I don't seem to remember your ever giving Molly much of a chance," said Frederick.

"But it's so co-o-o-ld in England," moaned Deborah.

James, in his bright, overbright clothes, a handsome well-preserved gent dressed for a southern summer, allowed himself the ironical snort of the oldster at youthful tactlessness, and his look at his wife and her husband apologised for Deborah. "And anyway," he insisted, "it *isn't* my style. You're quite wrong, Harriet. The opposite is true. People are brainwashed into believing family life is the best. But that's the past."

"If you don't like it, then why are you here?" demanded Harriet, much too belligerently for this pleasant morning scene. Then she blushed and exclaimed, "No, I didn't mean that!"

"No, of course you don't mean it," said Dorothy. "You're overtired."

"We are here because it's lovely," said a schoolgirl cousin of David's. She had an unhappy, or at least complicated, family background, and she had taken to spending her holidays here, her parents pleased she was having a taste of real family life. Her name was Bridget.

David and Harriet were exchanging long supportive humorous looks, as they often did, and had not heard the schoolgirl, who was now sending them pathetic glances.

"Come on, you two," said William, "tell Bridget she's welcome."

"What? What's the matter?" demanded Harriet.

William said, "Bridget has to be told by you that she is welcome. Well—we all do, from time to time," he added, in his facetious way, and could not help sending a look at his wife.

"Well, naturally you are welcome, Bridget," said David. He sent a glance to Harriet, who said at once, "But of course." She meant, That goes without saying; and the weight of a thousand marital discussions was behind it, causing Bridget to look from David to Harriet and back, and then around the whole family, saying, "When I get married, this is what I am going to do. I'm going to be like Harriet and David, and have a big house and a lot of children . . . and you'll all be welcome." She was fifteen, a plain dark plump girl who they all knew would shortly blossom and become beautiful. They told her so.

"It's natural," said Dorothy tranquilly. "You haven't any sort of a home really, so you value it."

"Something wrong with that logic," said Molly.

The schoolgirl looked around the table, at a loss.

"My mother means that you can only value something if you've experienced it," said David. "But I am the living proof that isn't so."

"If you're saying you didn't have a proper home," said Molly, "that's just nonsense."

"You had two," said James.

"I had my room," said David. "*My room*—that was home."

"Well, I suppose we must be grateful for that concession. I was not aware you felt deprived," said Frederick.

"I didn't, ever—I had my room."

They decided to shrug, and laugh.

"And you haven't even thought about the problems of educating them all," said Molly. "Not so far as we can see."

And now here was appearing that point of difference that the life in this house so successfully smoothed over. It went without saying that David had gone to private schools.

"Luke will start at the local school this year," said Harriet. "And Helen will start next year."

"Well, if that's good enough for you," said Molly.

"My three went to ordinary schools," said Dorothy, not letting this slide; but Molly did not accept the challenge. She remarked, "Well, unless James chips in to help . . ." thus making it clear that she and Frederick could not or would not contribute.

James said nothing. He did not even allow himself to look ironical.

"It's five years, six years, before we have to worry about the next stage of education for Luke and Helen," said Harriet, again sounding over-irritable.

Insisted Molly: "We put David down for his schools when he was born. And Deborah, too."

"Well," said Deborah, "why am I any better for my posh schools than Harriet—or anyone else?"

"It's a point," said James, who had paid for the posh schools.

"Not much of a point," said Molly.

William sighed, clowning it: "Deprived all the rest of us are. Poor William. Poor Sarah. Poor Bridget. Poor Harriet. Tell me, Molly, if I had been to posh schools would I get a decent job now?"

"That isn't the point," said Molly.

"She means you'd be happier unemployed or in a filthy job well educated than badly educated," said Sarah.

"I'm sorry," said Molly. "Public education is awful. It's getting worse. Harriet and David have got four children to educate. With more to come, apparently. How do you know James will be able to help you? Anything can happen in the world."

"Anything does, all the time," said William bitterly, but laughed to soften it.

Harriet moved distressfully in her chair, took Paul off her breast with a skill at concealing herself they all noted and admired, and said, "I don't want to have this conversation. It's a lovely morning. . . ."

"I'll help you, of course, within limits," said James.

"Oh, James . . ." said Harriet, "thank you . . . thank you. . . . Oh dear . . . why don't we go up to the woods? . . . We could take a picnic lunch."

The morning had slid past. It was midday. Sun struck the edges of the jolly red curtains, making them an intense orange, sending orange lozenges to glow on the table among cups, saucers, a bowl of fruit. The children had come down from the top of the house and were in the garden. The adults went to watch them from the windows. The garden continued neglected; there was never time for it. The lawn was patchily lush, and toys lay about. Birds sang in the shrubs, ignoring the children.

Little Jane, set down by Dorothy, staggered out to join the others. A group of children played noisily together, but she was too young, and strayed in and out of the game, in the private world of a two-year-old. They skilfully accommodated their game to her. The week before, Easter Sunday, this garden had had painted eggs hidden everywhere in it. A wonderful day, the children bringing in magical eggs from everywhere that Harriet and Dorothy and Bridget, the schoolgirl, had sat up half the night to decorate.

Harriet and David were together at the window, the baby in her arms. He put his arm around her. They exchanged a quick look, half guilty because of the irrepressible smiles on their faces, which they felt were probably going to exasperate the others.

"You two are incorrigible," said William. "They are hopeless," he said to the others. "Well, who's complaining? I'm not! Why don't we all go for that picnic?"

The house party filled five cars, children wedged in or on the adults' laps.

Summer was the same: two months of it, and again the family came and went, and came again. The schoolgirl was there all the time, poor Bridget, clinging fast to this miracle of a family. Rather, in fact, as Harriet and David did. Both more than once—seeing the girl's face, reverential, even awed, always on the watch as if she feared to miss some revelation of goodness or grace the moment she allowed her attention to lapse—saw themselves. Even uneasily saw themselves. It was too much . . . excessive. . . . Surely they should be saying to her, "Look here, Bridget, don't expect so much. Life isn't like that!" But life *is* like that, if you choose right: so why should they feel she couldn't have what they had so plentifully?

Even before the crowd gathered before the Christmas of 1973, Harriet was pregnant again. To her utter dismay, and David's. How could it have happened? They had been careful, particularly so because of their determination not to have any more children for a while. David tried to joke, "It's this room, I swear it's a baby-maker!"

They had put off telling Dorothy. She was not there, anyway, because Sarah had said it was unfair that Harriet got all the help. Harriet simply could not manage. One after another, three girls came to help; they had just left school and could not easily find work. They were not much good. Harriet believed she looked after them more than they her. They came or didn't come as the mood took them, and would sit around drinking tea with their girl-friends while Harriet toiled. She was frantic, exhausted . . . she was peevish; she lost her temper; she burst into tears. . . . David saw her sitting at the kitchen table, head in her hands, muttering that this new foetus was poisoning her: Paul lay whimpering in his pram, ignored. David took a fort-night's leave from his office to come home and help. They had known how much they owed Dorothy, but now knew it better— and that when she heard Harriet was pregnant again she would be angry. Very. And she would be right.

"It will all be easier when Christmas starts," wept Harriet.

"You can't be serious," said David, furious. "Of course they can't come this Christmas."

"But it is so easy when people are here, everyone helps me."

"Just for once we'll go to one of them," said David, but this idea did not live for more than five minutes: none of the other households could accommodate six extra people.

Harriet lay weeping on her bed. "But they must come, don't put them off—oh, David, please . . . at least it'll keep my mind off it."

He sat on his side of the bed watching her, uneasy, critical, trying not to be. Actually he would be pleased not to have the house full of people for three weeks, a month: it cost so much, and they were always short of money. He had taken on extra work, and here he was at home, a nursemaid.

"You simply have to get someone in to help, Harriet. You must try and keep one of them."

She burst out in indignation at the criticism. "That's not fair! You aren't here stuck with them—they aren't any good. I don't believe any of these girls have done an hour's work in their lives."

"They've been some help—even if it's only the washing-up."

Dorothy telephoned to say that both Sarah and Harriet were going to have to manage: she, Dorothy, needed a break. She was going home to her flat to please herself for a few weeks. Harriet was weeping, hardly able to speak. Dorothy could not get out of her what could possibly be wrong: she said, "Very well, I suppose I'll have to come, then."

She sat at the big table with David, Harriet, the four children there, too, and looked severely at Harriet. She had understood her daughter was pregnant again within half an hour of arriving. They could see from her set angry face that she had terrible things to say. "I'm your servant, I do the work of a servant in this house." Or, "You are very selfish, both of you. You are irresponsible." These words were in the air but were not spoken: they knew that if she allowed herself to begin she would not stop with this.

She sat at the head of the table—the position near the stove—stirring her tea, with one eye on baby Paul, who was fretful in his little chair and wanted to be cuddled. Dorothy, too, looked tired, and her grey hair was disordered: she had been going up to her room to tidy herself when she had been swallowed in embraces with Luke and Helen and Jane, who had missed her and knew that the crossness and impatience that had ruled the house would now be banished.

"You know that everyone is expecting to come here for Christmas," she demanded heavily, *not* looking at them.

"Oh yes, yes, yes," clamoured Luke and Helen, making a song and dance of it and rushing around the kitchen. "Oh yes, when are they coming? Is Tony coming? Is Robin coming? Is Anne coming?"

"Sit down," said David, sharp and cold, and they gave him astonished, hurt looks and sat.

"It's crazy," said Dorothy. She was flushed with the hot tea and with all the things she was forcing herself not to say.

"Of course everyone has to come," Harriet said, weeping— and ran out of the room.

"It's very important to her," said David apologetically.

"And not to you?" This was sarcastic.

"The thing is, I don't think Harriet is anywhere near herself," said David, and held his eyes on Dorothy's, to make her face him. But she would not.

"What does that mean, my mother isn't near herself?" enquired Luke, the six-year-old, ready to make a word game of it. Even, perhaps, a riddle. But he was perturbed. David put out his arm and Luke went to his father, stood close, looked up into his face.

"It's all right, Luke," said David.

"You've got to get someone in to help," said Dorothy.

"We have tried." David explained what had happened with the three amiable and indifferent girls.

"Doesn't surprise me. Who wants to do an honest job these days?" said Dorothy. "But you have to get someone. And I can tell you I didn't expect to end my days as your and Sarah's skivvy."

Here Luke and Helen gave their grandmother incredulous looks and burst into tears. After a pause, Dorothy controlled herself and began consoling them.

"All right, it's all right," she said. "And now I'm going to put Paul and Jane to bed. You two, Luke and Helen, can put yourselves to bed. I'll come up and say good night. And then your gran is off to bed. I'm tired."

The subdued children went off upstairs.

Harriet did not come down again that evening; her husband and her mother knew she was being sick. Which they were used to . . . but were not used to ill temper, tears, fretfulness.

When the children were in bed, David did some of the work he had brought home, made himself a sandwich, and was joined by Dorothy, who had come down to make herself tea. This time they did not exchange irritabilities: they were together in a companionable silence, like two old campaigners facing trials and difficulties.

Then David went up into the great shadowy bedroom, where lights from an upstairs window in a neighbouring house a good thirty yards away sent gleams and shadows on to the ceiling. He stood looking at the big bed where Harriet lay. Asleep? Baby Paul was lying asleep close to her, unwrapped. David cautiously leaned over, folded Paul into his cuddling blanket, took him to his room next door. He saw Harriet's eyes shine as she followed his movements.

He got into bed and, as always, slid out his arm so that she could put her head on to it and be gathered close to him.

But she said, "Feel this," and guided his hand to her stomach.

She was nearly three months pregnant.

This new baby had not yet shown signs of independent life, but now David felt a jolt under his hand, quite a hard movement.

"Can you be further along than you thought?" Once more he felt the thrust, and could not believe it.

Harriet was weeping again, and he felt, knowing of course this was unfair, that she was breaking the rules of some contract between them: tears and misery had not ever been on their agenda!

She felt rejected by him. They had always loved to lie here feeling a new life, greeting it. She had waited four times for the first little flutters, easily mistaken but then certain; the sensation that was as if a fish mouthed out a bubble; the small responses to her movements, her touch, and even—she was convinced—her thoughts.

This morning, lying in the dark before the children woke, she had felt a tapping in her belly, demanding attention. Disbelieving, she had half sat up, looking down at her still flat, if soft, stomach, and felt the imperative beat, like a small drum. She had been keeping herself on the move all day, so as not to feel these demands from the new being, unlike anything she had known before.

"You had better go and get Dr. Brett to check the dates," said David.

Harriet said nothing, feeling it was beside the point: she did not know why she felt this.

But she did go to Dr. Brett.

He said, "Well, perhaps I was out by a month—but if so, you have really been very careless, Harriet."

This scolding was what she was getting from everyone, and she flashed out, "Anyone can make a mistake."

He frowned as he felt the emphatic movements in her stomach, and remarked, "Well, there's nothing very much wrong with *that*, is there?" He looked dubious, however. He was a harassed, no longer young man, who, she had heard, had a difficult marriage. She had always felt rather superior to him. Now she felt at his mercy, and was looking up into that professionally reticent face as she lay there, under his hands, longing for him to say something else. What? *An explanation.*

"You'll have to take it easy," he said, turning away.

Behind his back, she muttered, "Take it easy yourself!" and chided herself, You bad-tempered *cow.*

Everyone arriving for Christmas was told Harriet was pregnant—it was a mistake—but now they were pleased, really. . . . But "Speak for yourselves," said Dorothy. People had to rally around, even more than they always did. Harriet was not to cook, do housework, do anything. She must be waited upon.

36

Each new person looked startled on hearing this news, then made jokes. Harriet and David came into rooms full of family, talking, who fell silent knowing they were there. They had been exchanging condemnations. Dorothy's role in keeping this household going was being given full credit. The pressure on David's salary—not, after all, a large one—was mentioned. Jokes were made about James's probable reception of the news. Then the teasing began. David and Harriet were commended for their fertility, and jokes were made about the influences of their bedroom. They responded to the jokes with relief. But all this jesting had an edge on it, and people were looking at the young Lovatts differently from the way they had done before. The quietly insistent patient quality that had brought them together, that had caused this house to come into being and had summoned all these unlikely people from various parts of England, and the world, too—James was coming from Bermuda, Deborah from the States, and even Jessica had promised to put in a brief appearance—this quality, whatever it was, this demand on life, which had been met in the past with respect (grudging or generous), was now showing its reverse side, in Harriet lying pale and unsociable on her bed, and then coming down determined to be one of the party but failing, and going upstairs again; in Dorothy's grim patience, for she worked from dawn to dusk and often in the night, too; and in the children's querulousness and demands for attention—particularly little Paul's.

Another girl came in from the village, found by Dr. Brett. She was, like the other three, pleasant, lazy, seeing nothing to be done unless her attention was directed to it, affronted by the amount of work needed by four children. She did, however, enjoy the people sitting around and talking, the sociable atmosphere, and in no time she was sharing meals and sitting around with them; she found it quite in order to be waited on by them. Everyone knew that she would find an excuse to leave when this delightful house party broke up.

Which it did, rather earlier than usual. It was not only Jessica (in her bright summer clothes that made no concession to the English winter except for a slight cardigan) who remembered people elsewhere who had been promised visits. Jessica took herself off, and Deborah with her. James followed. Frederick had to finish a book. The enraptured schoolgirl, Bridget, found Harriet lying down, her hands pressed into her stomach, tears running down her face, moaning from some pain she would not specify—and was so shocked she, too, wept and said she had always known it was too good to last, and went off back home to her mother, who had just remarried and did not really want her.

The girl who had come to help went home, and David looked for a trained nanny in London. He could not afford one, but James had said he would pay for it. Until Harriet was better, he said: uncharacteristically grumpy, he was making it clear he thought that Harriet had chosen this life and now should not expect everyone to foot the bill.

But they could not find a nanny: the nannies all wanted to go abroad with families who had a baby, or perhaps two; or to be in London. This small town, and the four children, with another coming, put them off.

Instead, Alice, a cousin of Frederick's, a widow down on her luck, came to help Dorothy. Alice was quick, fussy, nervous, like a little grey terrier. She had three grown-up children, and grandchildren, but said she did not want to be a nuisance to them, a remark that caused Dorothy to make dry remarks, which Harriet felt like accusations. Dorothy was not pleased to have a woman of her own age sharing authority, but it could not be helped. Harriet seemed unable to do anything much.

She went back to Dr. Brett, for she could not sleep or rest because of the energy of the foetus, which seemed to be trying to tear its way out of her stomach.

"Just look at that," she said as her stomach heaved up, convulsed, subsided. *"Five months."*

He made the usual tests, and said, "It's large for five months, but not abnormally so."

"Have you ever had a case like this before?" Harriet sounded sharp, peremptory, and the doctor gave her an annoyed look.

"I've certainly seen energetic babies before," he said shortly, and when she demanded, "At five months? Like this?" he refused to meet her—was dishonest, as she felt it. "I'll give you a sedative," he said. For her. But she thought of it as something to quiet the baby.

Now, afraid of asking Dr. Brett, she begged tranquillisers from friends, and from her sisters. She did not tell David how many she was taking, and this was the first time she had hidden anything from him. The foetus was quiet for about an hour after she dosed herself, and she was given a respite from the ceaseless battering and striving. It was so bad that she would cry out in pain. At night, David heard her moan, or whimper, but now he did not offer comfort, for it seemed that these days she did not find his arms around her any help.

"My *God*," she said, or grunted, or groaned, and then suddenly sat up, or scrambled out of bed and went doubled up out of the room, fast, escaping from the pain.

He had stopped putting his hand on her stomach, in the old companionable way, for what he felt there was beyond what he could manage with. It was not possible that such a tiny creature could be showing such fearful strength; and yet it did. And nothing he said seemed to reach Harriet, who, he felt, was possessed, had gone right away from him, in this battle with the foetus, which he could not share.

He might wake to watch her pacing the room in the dark, hour after hour. When she at last lay down, regulating her breathing, she would start up again, with an exclamation, and, knowing he was awake, would go downstairs to the big family room where she could stride up and down, groaning, swearing, weeping, without being observed.

As the Easter holiday approached and the two older women made remarks about getting the house ready, Harriet said, "They can't come. They can't possibly come."

"They'll expect it," said Dorothy.

"We can manage," said Alice.

"No," said Harriet.

Wails and protests from the children, and Harriet did not soften. This made Dorothy even more disapproving. Here she was, with Alice, two capable women, doing all the work, and the least Harriet could do . . .

"You're sure you don't want them to come?" asked David, who had been begged by the children to make her change her mind.

"Oh, do what you like," Harriet said.

But when Easter came, Harriet was proved right: it was not a success. Her strained, abstracted face as she sat there at her table, stiffly upright, braced for the next jolt, or jab, stopped conversation, spoiled the fun, the good times. "What have you got in there?" asked William, jocular but uneasy, seeing Harriet's stomach convulse. "A wrestler?"

"God only knows," said Harriet, and she was bitter, not joking. "How am I going to get through to July?" she demanded, in a low appalled voice. "I can't! I simply can't do it!"

They all—David, too—judged that she was simply exhausted because this baby was coming too soon. She must be humoured. Alone in her ordeal—and she had to be, she knew that, and did not blame her family for not accepting what she was being slowly forced to accept—she became silent, morose, suspicious of them all and their thoughts about her. The only thing that helped was to keep moving.

If a dose of some sedative kept the enemy—so she now thought of this savage thing inside her—quiet for an hour, then she made the most of the time, and slept, grabbing sleep to her, holding it, drinking it, before she leaped out of bed as it woke with a heave and a stretch that made her feel sick. She would clean the kitchen, the living-room, the stairs, wash windows, scrub cupboards, her whole body energetically denying the pain. She insisted that her mother and Alice let her work, and when they said there was no need to scrub the kitchen again, she said, "For the kitchen no, for me yes." By breakfast time she might have already worked for three or four hours, and looked hag-ridden. She took David to the station, and the two older children to school, then parked the car somewhere and walked. She almost ran through streets she hardly saw, hour after hour, until she understood she was causing comment. Then she took to driving a short way out of the town, where she walked along the country lanes, fast, sometimes running. People in passing cars would turn, amazed, to see this hurrying driven woman, white-faced, hair flying, open-mouthed, panting, arms clenched across her front. If they stopped to offer help, she shook her head and ran on.

Time passed. It did pass, though she was held in an order of time different from those around her—and not the pregnant woman's time either, which is slow, a calendar of the growth of the hidden being. Her time was endurance, containing pain. Phantoms and chimeras inhabited her brain. She would think, When the scientists make experiments, welding two kinds of animal together, of different sizes, then I suppose this is what the poor mother feels. She imagined pathetic botched creatures, horribly real to her, the products of a Great Dane or a borzoi with a little spaniel; a lion and a dog; a great cart horse and a little donkey; a tiger and a goat. Sometimes she believed hooves were cutting her tender inside flesh, sometimes claws.

In the afternoon, she collected the children from school, and, later, David from the station. She walked around the kitchen as suppers were eaten, encouraged the children to watch television, and then went up to the third floor where she hastened up and down the corridor.

The family could hear her swift heavy steps, up there, and did not let their eyes meet.

Time passed. It did pass. The seventh month was better, and this was because of the amount of drugs she took. Appalled at the distance that had grown up between her and her husband, between her and the children, her mother, Alice, she now planned her day for one thing: that she would seem to be normal between the hours of four, when Helen and Luke ended school, until eight or nine, when they went to bed. The drugs did not seem to be affecting her much: she was willing them to leave her alone and to reach the baby, the foetus—this creature with whom she was locked in a struggle to survive. And for those hours it was quiet, or if it showed signs of coming awake, and fighting her, she took another dose.

Oh how eager everyone was to welcome her back into the family, normal, herself: they ignored, because she wanted them to, her tenseness, her tiredness.

David would put his arms around her and say, "Oh, Harriet, you *are* all right?"

Two months to go.

"Yes, yes, I am. Really." And she silently addressed the being crouching in her womb: "Now you shut up or I'll take another pill." It seemed to her that it listened and understood.

A scene in the kitchen: family supper. Harriet and David commanded the head and foot of the table. Luke and Helen sat together on one side. Alice held little Paul, who could never get enough cuddling: he got so little from his mother. Jane sat near Dorothy's place, who was at the stove, ladle in her hand. Harriet looked at her mother, a large healthy woman in her fifties, with her bush of iron-grey curls, and her pink fresh face, and her large blue eyes "like lollipops"—a family joke—and thought, I'm as strong as she is. I'll survive. And she smiled at Alice, thin, wiry, tough, energetic, and thought again, These elderly women, look at them, they've survived everything.

Dorothy was filling their plates with vegetable soup. She sat down, at leisure, with her own plate. Bread was passed around, a big basket of it.

Happiness had returned and sat at the table with them—and Harriet's hand, unseen below the level of the table-top, was held over the enemy: *You be quiet.*

"A story," said Luke. "A story, Daddy."

On days when there was school tomorrow, the children had supper early and went up to bed. But on Fridays and Saturdays they ate with the grown-ups and a story was told during the meal.

Here, enclosed in the hospitable kitchen, it was warm and steamy with the smell of soup. Outside was a blustering night. May. The curtains were not drawn. A branch stretched across the window: a spring branch, full of pristine blossom, pale in the twilight, but the air that beat on the panes had been blasted down south from some iceberg or snow-field. Harriet was spooning in soup, and broke hunks of bread into it. Her appetite was enormous, insatiable—so bad she was ashamed and raided the fridge when no one could see her. She would interrupt her nocturnal peregrinations to stuff into herself anything she could find to eat. She even had secret caches like an alcoholic's hoards, only it was food: chocolate, bread, pies.

David began, "Two children, a boy and a girl, set off one day to have an adventure in the forest. They went a long way into the forest. It was hot outside, but under the trees it was cool. They saw a deer lying down, resting. Birds flitted about and sang to them."

David stopped to eat soup. Helen and Luke sat with their

43

eyes on his face, motionless. Jane listened, too, but differently. Four years old: she looked to see how they took in the story, and copied them, fixing her eyes on her father.

"Do the birds sing to us?" enquired Luke doubtfully, frowning. He had a strong, severe face; and, as always, he demanded the truth. "When we are in the garden and the birds sing, are they singing to us?"

"Of course not, silly," said Helen. "It was a magic forest."

"Of course they sing to you," said Dorothy firmly.

The children, first hunger appeased, sat with their spoons in their hands, wide eyes on their father. Harriet's heart oppressed her: it was their open trustfulness, their helplessness. The television was on: a professionally cool voice was telling about some murders in a London suburb. She lumbered over to turn it off, plodded back, served herself more soup, piled in the bread. . . . She listened to David's voice, tonight the storyteller's voice, so often heard in the kitchen, hers, Dorothy's—

"When the children got hungry, they found a bush covered with chocolate sweets. Then they found a pool made of orange juice. They were sleepy. They lay under a bush near the friendly deer. When they woke up, they said thank you to the deer and went on.

"Suddenly the little girl found she was alone. She and her brother had lost each other. She wanted to go home. She did not know which way to walk. She was looking for another friendly deer, or a sparrow, or any bird, to tell her where she was and show her the way out of the forest. She wandered about for a long time, and then she was thirsty again. She bent over a pool wondering if it would be orange juice, but it was water, clear pure forest water, and it tasted of plants and stones. She drank, from her hands." Here the two older children reached for their glasses and drank. Jane interlaced her fingers to form a cup.

"She sat there by the pool. Soon it would be dark. She bent

44

over the pool to see if there was a fish who could tell her the way out of the forest, but she saw something she didn't expect. It was a girl's face, and she was looking straight up at her. It was a face she had never seen in her whole life. This strange girl was smiling, but it was a nasty smile, not friendly, and the little girl thought this other girl was going to reach up out of the water and pull her down into it . . ."

A heavy, shocked, indrawn breath from Dorothy, who felt this was too frightening at bedtime.

But the children sat frozen with attention. Little Paul, grizzling on Alice's lap, earned from Helen "Be quiet, shut *up.*"

"Phyllis—that was the little girl's name—had never seen such frightening eyes."

"Is that Phyllis in my nursery school?" asked Jane.

"No," said Luke.

"No," said Helen.

David had stopped. Apparently for inspiration. He was frowning, had an abstracted look, as if he had a headache. As for Harriet, she was wanting to cry out, "Stop—stop it! You are talking about me—this is what you are feeling about me!" She could not believe that David did not see it.

"What happened then?" asked Luke. "What happened exactly?"

"Wait," said David. "Wait, my soup . . ." He ate.

"I know what happened," said Dorothy firmly. "Phyllis decided to leave that nasty pool *at once.* She ran fast along a path until she bumped into her brother. He was looking for her. They held each other's hands and they ran out of the forest and they ran safely home."

"That was it, exactly," said David. He was smiling ruefully, but looked bemused.

"And that was what really really happened, Daddy?" demanded Luke, anxious.

"Absolutely," said David.

"Who was that girl in the pool, who was she?" demanded Helen, looking from her father to her mother.

"Oh just a magic girl," said David casually. "I have no idea. She just materialised."

"What's materialised?" asked Luke, saying the word with difficulty.

"It's bedtime," said Dorothy.

"But what is materialised?" Luke insisted.

"We haven't had any pudding!" cried Jane.

"There's no pudding, there's fruit," said Dorothy.

"What is materialised, Daddy?" Luke anxiously persisted.

"It is when something that wasn't there suddenly is there."

"But why, why is it?" wailed Helen, distressed.

Dorothy said, "Upstairs, children."

Helen took an apple, Luke another, and Jane lifted some bread off her mother's plate with a quick, conscious, mischievous smile. She had not been upset by the story.

The three children went noisily up the stairs, and baby Paul looked after them, excluded, his face puckering, ready to cry.

Alice swiftly got up with him and went after the children, saying, "No one told me stories when I was little!" It was hard to tell whether this was a complaint or, "and I'm better for it."

Suddenly, Luke appeared on the landing. "Is everyone coming for the summer holidays?"

David glanced worriedly at Harriet—then away. Dorothy looked steadily at her daughter.

"Yes," said Harriet weakly. "Of course."

Luke called up the stairs, "She said, 'Of course'!"

Dorothy said, "You will have just had this baby."

"It's up to you and Alice," said Harriet. "If you feel you can't cope, then you must say so."

"It seems to me that I cope," said Dorothy, dry.

"Yes, I know," said David quickly. "You're marvellous."

"And you don't know what you would have done—"

"Don't," said David. And to Harriet: "Much better that we put things off, and have them all at Christmas."

"The children will be so disappointed," said Harriet.

This did not sound like her old insistence: it was flat and indifferent. Her husband and her mother examined her curiously—so Harriet felt their inspection of her, detached, unkind. She said grimly, "Well, perhaps this baby will be born early. Surely it must." She laughed painfully, and then suddenly she got up, exclaiming, "I *must* move, I have to!" and began her dogged, painful hour-after-hour walk back and forth, up and down.

She went to Dr. Brett at eight months and asked him to induce the baby.

He looked critically at her and said, "I thought you didn't believe in it."

"I don't. But this is different."

"Not that I can see."

"It's because you don't want to. It's not you who is carrying this—" She cut off *monster*, afraid of antagonising him. "Look," she said, trying to sound calm, but her voice was angry and accusing, "would you say I was an unreasonable woman? Hysterical? Difficult? Just a pathetic hysterical woman?"

"I would say that you are utterly worn out. Bone tired. You never did find being pregnant easy, did you? Have you forgotten? I've had you sitting here through four pregnancies, with all kinds of problems—all credit to you, you put up with everything very well."

"But it's not the same thing, it is *absolutely* different, I don't understand why you can't see it. Can't you *see* it?" She thrust out her stomach, which was heaving and—as she felt it—seething as she sat there.

The doctor looked dubiously at her stomach, sighed, and wrote her a prescription for more sedatives.

No, he couldn't see it. Rather, he wouldn't—that was the

point. Not only he, but all of them, they *wouldn't* see how different this was.

And as she walked, strode, ran along the country lanes, she fantasised that she took the big kitchen knife, cut open her own stomach, lifted out the child—and when they actually set eyes on each other, after this long blind struggle, what would she see?

Soon, nearly a month early, the pains began. Once she started, labour had always gone quickly. Dorothy rang David in London, and at once took Harriet into hospital. For the first time, Harriet had insisted on a hospital, surprising everyone.

By the time she was there, there were strong wrenching pains, worse, she knew, than ever in the past. The baby seemed to be fighting its way out. She was bruised—she knew it; inside she must be one enormous black bruise . . . and no one would ever know.

When at last the moment came when she could be given oblivion, she cried out, "Thank God, thank God, it's over at last!" She heard a nurse saying, "This one's a real little toughie, look at him." Then a woman's voice was saying, "Mrs. Lovatt, Mrs. Lovatt, are you with us? Come back to us! Your husband is here, dear. You've a healthy boy."

"A real little wrestler," said Dr. Brett. "He came out fighting the whole world."

She raised herself with difficulty, because the lower half of her body was too sore to move. The baby was put into her arms. Eleven pounds of him. The others had not been more than seven pounds. He was muscular, yellowish, long. It seemed as if he were trying to stand up, pushing his feet into her side.

"He's a funny little chap," said David, and he sounded dismayed.

He was not a pretty baby. He did not look like a baby at all. He had a heavy-shouldered hunched look, as if he were crouching there as he lay. His forehead sloped from his eyebrows to his crown. His hair grew in an unusual pattern from the double crown where started a wedge or triangle that came low on the forehead, the hair lying forward in a thick yellowish stubble, while the side and back hair grew downwards. His hands were thick and heavy, with pads of muscle in the palms. He opened his eyes and looked straight up into his mother's face. They were focussed greeny-yellow eyes, like lumps of soapstone. She had been waiting to exchange looks with the creature who, she had been sure, had been trying to hurt her, but there was no recognition there. And her heart contracted with pity for him: poor little beast, his mother disliking him so much . . . But she heard herself say nervously, though she tried to laugh, "He's like a troll, or a goblin or something." And she cuddled him, to make up. But he was stiff and heavy.

"Come, Harriet," said Dr. Brett, annoyed with her. And she thought, I've been through this with Dr. bloody Brett four times and it's always been marvellous, and now he's like a schoolmaster.

She bared her breast and offered the child her nipple. The nurses, the doctor, her mother, and her husband stood watching, with the smiles that this moment imposed. But there was none of the atmosphere of festival, of achievement, no champagne; on the contrary, there was a strain in everyone, apprehension. A strong, sucking reflex, and then hard gums clamped down on her nipple, and she winced. The child looked at her and bit, hard.

"*Well*," said Harriet, trying to laugh, removing him.

"Try him a little more," said the nurse.

He was not crying. Harriet held him out, challenging the nurse with her eyes to take him. The nurse, mouth tight with disapproval, took the baby, and he was put unprotesting in his cot. He had not cried since he was born, except for a first roar of protest, or perhaps surprise.

The four children were brought in to see their new brother

49

in the hospital ward. The two other women who shared the room with her had got out of bed and taken their babies to a day-room. Harriet had refused to get out of bed. She told the doctors and nurses she needed time for her internal bruises to heal; she said this almost defiantly, carelessly, indifferent to their critical looks.

David stood at the end of the bed, holding baby Paul. Harriet yearned for this baby, this little child, from whom she had been separated so soon. She loved the look of him, the comical soft little face, with soft blue eyes—like bluebells, she thought— and his soft little limbs . . . it was as if she were sliding her hands along them, and then enclosing his feet in her palms. A real baby, a real little child . . .

The three older children stared down at the newcomer who was so different from them all: of a different substance, so it seemed to Harriet. Partly this was because she was still respond- ing to the look of him with her memories of his difference in the womb, but partly it was because of his heavy, sallow lump- ishness. And then there was this strange head of his, sloping back from the eyebrow ridges.

"We are going to call him Ben," said Harriet.

"Are we?" said David.

"Yes, it suits him."

Luke on one side, Helen on the other, took Ben's small hands, and said, "Hello, Ben." "Hello, Ben." But the baby did not look at them.

Jane, the four-year-old, took one of his feet in her hand, then in her two hands, but he vigorously kicked her away.

Harriet found herself thinking, I wonder what the mother would look like, the one who would welcome this—alien.

She stayed in bed a week—that is, until she felt she could manage the struggle ahead—and then went home with her new child.

That night, in the connubial bedroom, she sat up against a stack of pillows, nursing the baby. David was watching.

Ben sucked so strongly that he emptied the first breast in less than a minute. Always, when a breast was nearly empty, he ground his gums together, and so she had to snatch him away before he could begin. It looked as if she were unkindly depriving him of the breast, and she heard David's breathing change. Ben roared with rage, fastened like a leech to the other nipple, and sucked so hard she felt that her whole breast was disappearing down his throat. This time, she left him on the nipple until he ground his gums hard together and she cried out, pulling him away.

"He's extraordinary," said David, giving her the support she needed.

"Yes, he *is*, he's absolutely *not* ordinary."

"But he's all right, he's just . . ."

"A normal healthy fine baby," said Harriet, bitter, quoting the hospital.

David was silent: it was this anger, this bitterness in her that he could not handle.

She was holding Ben up in the air. He was wrestling, fighting, struggling, crying in his characteristic way, which was a roar or a bellow, while he went yellowish white with anger—not red, like a normal cross baby.

When she held him to get up the wind, he seemed to be standing in her arms, and she felt weak with fear at the thought that this strength had so recently been inside her, and she at its mercy. For months, he had been fighting to get out, just as now he fought in her grasp to become independent.

When she laid him in his cot, which she was always glad to do because her arms ached so badly, he bellowed out his rage, but soon lay quiet, not sleeping, fully alert, his eyes focussed, and his whole body flexing and unflexing with a strong pushing movement of heels and head she was familiar with: it was what had made her feel she was being torn apart when he was inside her.

She went back into bed beside David. He put out his arm, so that she could lie by him, inside it, but she felt treacherous and untruthful, for he would not have liked what she was thinking.

Soon she was exhausted with feeding Ben. Not that he did not thrive: he did. He was two pounds over his birth weight when he was a month, which was when he would have been less than a week old if he had gone full term.

Her breasts were painful. Making more milk than they ever had had to do, her chest swelled into two bursting white globes long before the next feed was due. But Ben was already roaring for it, and she fed him, and he drained every drop in two or three minutes. She felt the milk being dragged in streams from her. Now he had begun something new: he had taken to interrupting the fierce sucking several times during a feed, and bringing his gums together in the hard grinding movement that made her cry out in pain. His small cold eyes seemed to her malevolent.

"I'm going to put him on the bottle," she said to Dorothy, who was watching this battle with the look, it seemed to Harriet, everyone had when watching Ben. She was absolutely still and intent, fascinated, almost hypnotised, but there was repugnance there, too. And fear?

Harriet had expected her mother to protest with "But he's only five weeks old!"—but what Dorothy said was "Yes, you must, or you'll be ill." A little later, watching Ben roar, and twist and fight, she remarked, "They'll all be coming soon for the summer." She spoke in a way new to her, as if listening to what she said and afraid of what she might say. Harriet recognised it, for this was how she felt saying anything at all. So do people speak whose thoughts are running along secretly in channels they would rather other people did not know about.

On that same day, Dorothy came into the bedroom where Harriet fed Ben, and saw Harriet pulling the child clear of breasts that had bruises all around the nipples. She said, "Do it. Do it now. I've bought the bottles, and the milk. I'm sterilising the bottles now."

"Yes, wean him," said David, agreeing at once. But she had fed the other four for months, and there had been hardly a bottle in the house.

The adults, Harriet and David, Dorothy and Alice, were around the big table, the children having gone up to bed, and Harriet tried Ben with the bottle. He emptied it in a moment, while his body clenched and unclenched, his knees up in his stomach, then extended like a spring. He roared at the empty bottle.

"Give him another," said Dorothy, and set about preparing one.

"What an appetite," said Alice socially, trying hard, but she looked frightened.

Ben emptied the second bottle: he was supporting it with his two fists, by himself. Harriet barely needed to touch it.

"Neanderthal baby," said Harriet.

"Oh come on, poor little chap," said David, uneasy.

"Oh God, David," said Harriet, "poor Harriet is more like it."

"All right, all right—the genes have come up with something special this time."

"But what, that's the point," said Harriet. "*What* is he?"

The other three said nothing—or, rather, said by their silence that they would rather not face the implications of it.

"All right," said Harriet, "let's say he has a healthy appetite, if that makes everyone happy."

Dorothy took the fighting creature from Harriet, who collapsed exhausted back in her chair. Dorothy's face changed as she felt the clumsy weight of the child, the intransigence, and she shifted her position so that Ben's pistoning legs could not reach her.

Soon Ben was taking in twice the amount of food recommended for his age, or stage: ten or more bottles a day.

He got a milk infection, and Harriet took him to Dr. Brett.

"A breast-fed baby shouldn't get infections," he said.

"He's not breast-fed."

"That's not like you, Harriet! How old is he?"

"Two months," said Harriet. She opened her dress and showed her breasts, still making milk, as if they responded to Ben's never appeased appetite. They were bruised black all around the nipples.

Dr. Brett looked at the poor breasts in silence, and Harriet looked at him: his decent, concerned doctor's face confronting a problem beyond him.

"Naughty baby," he conceded, and Harriet laughed out loud in astonishment.

Dr. Brett reddened, met her eyes briefly in acknowledgement of her reproach, and then looked away.

"All I need is a prescription for diarrhoea," said Harriet. She added deliberately, staring at him, willing him to look at her, "After all, I don't want to kill the nasty little brute."

He sighed, took off his glasses, and rubbed them slowly. He was frowning, but not in disapproval of her. He said, "It is not abnormal to take a dislike to a child. I see it all the time. Unfortunately."

Harriet said nothing, but she was smiling unpleasantly, and knew it.

"Let me have a look at him."

Harriet took Ben out of the pram, and laid him on the table. At once he turned on to his stomach and tried to get himself on all fours. He actually succeeded for a moment before collapsing.

She looked steadily at Dr. Brett, but he turned away to his desk to write a prescription.

"There's obviously nothing much wrong with him," he said, with the same baffled, offended note that Ben did bring out of people.

"Have you ever seen a two-month baby do that?" she insisted.

"No. I must admit I haven't. Well, let me know how you get on."

The news had flown around the family that the new baby was successfully born, and everything was all right. Meaning that Harriet was. A lot of people wrote and rang, saying they were looking forward to the summer holidays. They said, "We are longing to see the new baby." They said, "Is little Paul still as delicious as he was?" They arrived bringing wine and summer produce from all over the country, and all kinds of people stood bottling fruit and making jams and chutneys with Alice and Dorothy. A crowd of children played in the garden or were taken off to the woods for picnics. Little Paul, so cuddlesome and funny, was always on somebody's lap, and his laugh was heard everywhere: this was his real nature, overshadowed by Ben and his demands.

Because the house was so full, the older children were in one room. Ben was already in a cot with high wooden slatted sides, where he spent his time pulling himself up to a sitting position, falling, rolling over, pulling himself up. . . . This cot was put in the room where the older children were, in the hope that Ben would be made social, friendly, by his siblings. It was not a success. He ignored them, would not respond to their advances, and his crying—or, rather, bellowing—made Luke shout at him, "Oh *shut up!*"—but then he burst into tears at his own unkindness. Helen, at the age to cherish a baby, tried to hold Ben, but he was too strong. Then all the older children in the house were put into the attic, where they could make as much noise as they wanted, and Ben went back into his own room, "the baby's room"—and from there they heard his grunts and snuffles and roars of frustration as he tried some feat of strength and fell down.

The new baby had of course been offered to everyone to hold, when they asked, but it was painful to see how their faces changed confronting this phenomenon. Ben was always quickly handed back. Harriet came into the kitchen one day and heard her sister Sarah say to a cousin, "That Ben gives me the creeps. He's like a goblin or a dwarf or something. I'd rather have poor Amy any day."

This afflicted Harriet with remorse: poor Ben, whom no one could love. She certainly could not! And David, the good father, hardly touched him. She lifted Ben from his cot, so much like a cage, and put him on the big bed, and sat with him. "Poor Ben, poor Ben," she crooned, stroking him. He clutched her shirt with both hands, pulled himself up, and stood on her thigh. The hard little feet hurt her. She tried to cuddle him, persuade him to soften against her. . . . Soon she gave up, put him back in his pen, or cage . . . a roar of frustration because he had been put down, and she held out her hands to him, "Poor Ben, dear Ben," and he grasped her hands and pulled himself up and stood grunting and roaring with triumph. Four months old . . . He was like an angry, hostile little troll.

She did make a point of going to him every day when the other children were out of the way, and taking him to the big bed for a time of petting and play, as she had with all of them. Never, not once, did he subside into a loving moment. He resisted, he strove, he fought—and then he turned his head and closed his jaws over her thumb. Not as an ordinary baby will, in the sucking bite that relieves the pain of teething, or explores the possibilities of a mouth, tongue: she felt her bone bend, and saw his cold triumphant grin.

She heard herself say, "You aren't going to do me in, I won't let you."

But for a while she did try hard to make him ordinary. She took him down into the big living-room where all the family were, and put him into the play-pen there—until his presence affected people, and they tended to go away. Or she took him to the table in her arms, as she had done with the others—but could not hold him, he was too strong.

In spite of Ben, the summer holidays were wonderful. Again, there were two months of it. Again, David's father, briefly descending, gave them a cheque, and they could not have managed without. "It is like being in the middle of some bloody great fruit pudding, this house," said James. "God knows how you do it."

But afterwards, when Harriet thought of those holidays, what she remembered was how they all looked at Ben. There would be a long thoughtful stare, puzzled, even anxious; but then came fear, though everyone tried to conceal it. There was horror, too: which is what Harriet felt, more and more. Soon she was shutting Ben up in his room away from everyone. He did not seem to mind, or even to notice. It was hard to make out what he did think of other people.

Harriet lay inside David's arms one night before sleeping, talking over the day, as they always did, and she remarked, out of a current of thoughts about the summer, "Do you know what this house is good for? What people come for? It's for a good time, that's all."

He was surprised. Even—she felt—shocked. "But what else do we do it for?" he enquired.

"I don't know," she said, sounding helpless. Then she turned in to his embrace, and he held her while she wept. They had not yet resumed love-making. This had never happened before. Making love during pregnancy, and very soon after pregnancy— this had never been a problem. But now they were both thinking, That creature arrived when we were being as careful as we knew how—suppose another like him comes? For they both felt—secretly, they were ashamed of the thoughts they had about Ben—that he had willed himself to be born, had invaded their ordinariness, which had no defences against him or anything like him. But not making love was not only a strain for them both, it was a barrier, because they had to be reminded continually of what threatened them . . . so they felt.

Then something bad happened. Just after all the family had gone away, as the school term began, Paul went into Ben's room by himself. Of all the children, he was the most fascinated by Ben. Dorothy and Alice, who were together in the kitchen, Harriet having gone off to take the older ones to school, heard screams. They ran upstairs to find that Paul had put his hand in to Ben through the cot bars, and Ben had grabbed the hand and pulled Paul hard against the bars, bending the arm deliberately backwards. The two women freed Paul. They did not bother to scold Ben, who was crowing with pleasure and achievement. Paul's arm was badly sprained.

No one felt like saying to the children, "Be careful of Ben." But there was no need after the incident with Paul's arm. That evening the children heard what had happened, but did not look at their parents and Dorothy and Alice. They did not look at each other. They stood silent, heads bent. This told the adults that the children's attitudes to Ben were already formed: they had discussed Ben and knew what to think about him. Luke, Helen, and Jane went away upstairs silently, and it was a bad moment for the parents.

Alice said, watching them, "Poor little things."

Dorothy said, "It's a shame."

Harriet felt that these two women, these two elderly, tough, seasoned survivors, were condemning her, Harriet, out of their vast experience of life. She glanced at David, and saw he felt the same. Condemnation, and criticism, and dislike: Ben seemed to cause these emotions, bring them forth out of people into the light. . . .

The day after this incident, Alice announced that she felt she was no longer needed in this house, she would go back to her own life: she was sure Dorothy could manage. After all, Jane was going to school now. Jane would not have gone to school this year, a proper school, all day, for another year: they had sent her early. Precisely because of Ben, though no one had said it. Alice left, with no suggestion it was because of Ben. But she had told Dorothy, who had told the parents, that Ben gave her the horrors. He must be a changeling. Dorothy, always sensible, calm, matter-of-fact, had laughed at her. "Yes, I laughed at her," she reported. Then, grim, "But why did I?"

David and Harriet conferred, in the low, almost guilty, incredulous voices that Ben seemed to impose. This baby was not six months old yet . . . he was going to destroy their family life. He was already destroying it. They would have to make sure that he was in his room at mealtimes and when the children were downstairs with the adults. Family times, in short.

Now Ben was almost always in his room, like a prisoner. He outgrew his barred cot at nine months: Harriet caught him just as he was about to fall over the top. A small bed, an ordinary one, was put into his room. He walked easily, holding on to the walls, or a chair. He had never crawled, had pulled himself straight up on to his feet. There were toys all over the floor— or, rather, the fragments of them. He did not play with them: he banged them on the floor or the walls until they broke. The day he stood alone, by himself, without holding on, he roared out his triumph. All the other children had laughed, chuckled, and wanted to be loved, admired, praised, on reaching this moment of achievement. This one did not. It was a cold triumph, and he staggered about, eyes gleaming with hard pleasure, while he ignored his mother. Harriet often wondered what he saw when he looked at her: nothing in his touch or his look ever seemed to say, This is my mother.

One early morning, something took Harriet quickly out of her bed into the baby's room, and there she saw Ben balanced on the window-sill. It was high—heaven only knew how he had got up there! The window was open. In a moment he would have fallen out of it. Harriet was thinking, What a pity I came in . . . and refused to be shocked at herself. Heavy bars were put in, and there Ben would stand on the sill, gripping the bars and shaking them, and surveying the outside world, letting out his thick, raucous cries. All the Christmas holidays he was kept in that room. It was extraordinary how people, asking—cautiously—"How is Ben?" and hearing, "Oh, he's all right," did not ask again. Sometimes a yell from Ben loud enough to reach downstairs silenced a conversation. Then the frown appeared on their faces that Harriet dreaded, waiting for it: she knew it masked some comment or thought that could not be voiced.

And so the house was not the same; there was a constraint and a wariness in everybody. Harriet knew that sometimes people went up to look at Ben, out of the fearful, uneasy curiosity he evoked, when she was out of the way. She knew when they had seen him, because of the way they looked at her afterwards. As if I were a criminal! she raged to herself. She spent far too much of her time quietly seething, but did not seem able to stop. Even David, she believed, condemned her. She said to him, "I suppose in the old times, in primitive societies, this was how they treated a woman who'd given birth to a freak. As if it was her fault. But we are supposed to be civilised!"

He said, in the patient, watchful way he now had with her, "You exaggerate everything."

"That's a good word—for this situation! Congratulations! Exaggerate!"

"Oh God, Harriet," he said differently, helplessly, "don't let's do this—if *we* don't stand together, then . . ."

It was at Easter that the schoolgirl Bridget, who had returned to see if this miraculous kingdom of everyday life was perhaps still there, enquired, "What is wrong with him? Is he a mongol?"

"Down's syndrome," said Harriet. "No one calls it mongol now. But no, he's not."

"What's wrong with him, then?"

"Nothing at all," said Harriet airily. "As you can see for yourself."

Bridget went away, and never came back.

The summer holidays again. It was 1975. There were fewer guests: some had written or rung to say they could not afford the train fare, or the petrol. "Any excuse is better than none," remarked Dorothy.

"But people are hard up," said David.

"They weren't so hard up before that they couldn't afford to come and live here for weeks at a time at your expense."

Ben was over a year old now. He had not said one word yet, but in other ways he was more normal. Now it was difficult to keep him in his room. Children playing in the garden heard his thick, angry cries, and saw him up on the sill trying to push aside his bars.

So he came out of his little prison and joined them downstairs. He seemed to know that he ought to be like them. He would stand, head lowered, watching how everyone talked, and laughed, sitting around the big table; or sat talking in the living-room, while the children ran in and out. His eyes were on one face, then another: whomever he was looking at became conscious of that insistent gaze and stopped talking; or turned a back, or a shoulder, so as not to have to see him. He could silence a room full of people just by being there, or disperse them: they went off making excuses.

Towards the end of the holidays, someone came bringing a dog, a little terrier. Ben could not leave it alone. Wherever the dog was, Ben followed. He did not pet it, or stroke it: he stood staring. One morning when Harriet came down to start breakfast for the children, the dog was lying dead on the kitchen floor. It had had a heart attack? Suddenly sick with suspicion, she rushed up to see if Ben was in his room: he was squatting on his bed, and when she came in, he looked up and laughed, but soundlessly, in his way, which was like a baring of the teeth. He had opened his door, gone quietly past his sleeping parents, down the stairs, found the dog, killed it, and gone back up again, quietly, into his room, and shut the door . . . all that, by himself! She locked Ben in: if he could kill a dog, then why not a child?

When she went down again, the children were crowding around the dead dog. And then the adults came, and it was obvious what they thought.

Of course it was impossible—a small child killing a lively dog. But officially the dog's death remained a mystery; the vet said it had been strangled. This business of the dog spoiled what was left of the holidays, and people went off home early.

Dorothy said, "People are going to think twice about coming again."

Three months later, Mr. McGregor, the old grey cat, was killed in the same way. He had always been afraid of Ben, and kept out of reach. But Ben must have stalked him, or found him sleeping.

At Christmas the house was half empty.

It was the worst year of Harriet's life, and she was not able to care that people avoided them. Every day was a long nightmare. She woke in the morning unable to believe she would ever get through to the evening. Ben was always on his feet, and had to be watched every second. He slept very little. He spent most of the night standing on his window-sill, staring into the garden, and if Harriet looked in on him, he would turn and give her a long stare, alien, chilling: in the half dark of the room he really did look like a little troll or a hobgoblin crouching there. If he was locked in during the day, he screamed and bellowed so that the whole house resounded with it, and they were all afraid the police would arrive. He would suddenly, for no reason she could see, take off and run into the garden, and then out the gate and into the street. One day, she ran a mile or more after him, seeing only that stubby squat little figure going through traffic lights, ignoring cars that hooted and people who screamed warnings at him. She was weeping, panting, half crazed, desperate to get to him before something terrible happened, but she was praying, Oh, do run him over, do, yes, *please.* . . . She caught up with him just before a main road, grabbed him, and held the fighting child with all her strength. He was spitting and hissing, while he jerked like a monster fish in her arms. A taxi went by; she called to it, she pushed the child in, and got in after him, holding him fast by an arm that seemed would break with his flailing about and fighting.

What could be done? Again she went to Dr. Brett, who examined him and said he was physically in order.

Harriet described his behaviour and the doctor listened.

From time to time, a well-controlled incredulity appeared on his face, and he kept his eyes down, fiddling with pencils.

"You can ask David, ask my mother," said Harriet.

"He's a hyperactive child—that's how they are described these days, I believe," said old-fashioned Dr. Brett. She went to him because he was old-fashioned.

At last he did look at her, not evading her.

"What do you expect me to do, Harriet? Drug him silly? Well, I am against it."

She was crying inwardly, Yes, yes, yes, that's exactly what I want! But she said, "No, of course not."

"He's physically normal for eighteen months. He's very strong and active of course, but he's always been that. You say he's not talking? But that's not unusual. Wasn't Helen a late talker? I believe she was?"

"Yes," said Harriet.

She took Ben home. Now he was locked into his room each night, and there were heavy bars on the door as well. Every second of his waking hours, he was watched. Harriet watched him while her mother managed everything else.

David said, "What is the point of thanking you, Dorothy? It seems everything has gone a long way beyond thank-yous."

"Everything has gone a long way beyond. Period." Said Dorothy.

Harriet was thin, red-eyed, haggard. Once again she was bursting into tears over nothing at all. The children kept out of her way. Tact? Were they afraid of her? Dorothy suggested staying alone with Ben for a week in August while the family went off together somewhere.

Neither Harriet nor David would normally have wanted to go anywhere, for they loved their home. And what about the family coming for the summer?

"I haven't noticed any rush to book themselves in," said Dorothy.

They went to France, with the car. For Harriet it was all happiness: she felt she had been given back her children. She could not get enough of them, nor they of her. And Paul, her baby whom Ben had deprived her of, the wonderful three-year-old, enchanting, a charmer—was her baby again. They were a family still! Happiness . . . they could hardly believe, any of them, that Ben could have taken so much away from them.

When they got home, Dorothy was very tired and she had a bad bruise on her forearm and another on her cheek. She did not say what had happened. But when the children had gone to bed on the first evening, she said to Harriet and David, "I have to talk—no, sit down and listen."

They sat with her at the kitchen table.

"You two are going to have to face it. Ben has got to go into an institution."

"But he's normal," said Harriet, grim. "The doctor says he is."

"He may be normal for what he is. But he is not normal for what we are."

"What kind of institution would take him?"

"There must be something," said Dorothy, and began to cry.

Now began a time when every night Harriet and David lay awake talking about what could be done. They were making love again, but it was not the same. "This must be what women felt before there was birth control," Harriet said. "Terrified. They waited for every period, and when it came it meant reprieve for a month. But they weren't afraid of giving birth to a troll."

While they talked, they always listened for sounds from "the baby's room"—words they never used now, for they hurt. What was Ben doing that they had not believed him capable of? Pulling those heavy steel bars aside?

"The trouble is, you get used to hell," said Harriet. "After a day with Ben I feel as if nothing exists but him. As if nothing has ever existed. I suddenly realise I haven't remembered the others for hours. I forgot their supper yesterday. Dorothy went to the pictures, and I came down and found Helen cooking their supper."

"It didn't hurt them."

"She's *eight*."

Having been reminded, by the week in France, of what their family life really was, could be, Harriet was determined not to let it all go. She found she was again silently addressing Ben: "I'm not going to let you destroy us, you won't destroy me. . . ."

She was set on another real Christmas, and wrote and tele-

THE FIFTH CHILD

phoned to everyone. She made a point of saying that Ben was "much better, these days."

Sarah asked if it would be "all right" to bring Amy. This meant that she had heard—everyone had—about the dog, and the cat.

"It'll be all right if we are careful never to leave Amy alone with Ben," said Harriet, and Sarah, after a long silence, said, "My God, Harriet, we've been dealt a bad hand, haven't we?" "I suppose so," said Harriet, but she was rejecting this submission to being a victim of fate. Sarah, yes; with her marital problems, and her mongol child—yes. But she, Harriet, in the same boat?

She said to her own children, "Please look after Amy. Never leave her alone with Ben."

"Would he hurt Amy the way he hurt Mr. McGregor?" asked Jane.

"He killed Mr. McGregor," Luke said fiercely. "He *killed* him."

"And the poor dog," said Helen. Both children were accusing Harriet.

"Yes," said Harriet, "he might. That's why we have to watch her all the time."

The children, the way they did these days, were looking at each other, excluding her, in some understanding of their own. They went off, without looking at her.

The Christmas, with fewer people, was nevertheless festive and noisy, a success; but Harriet found herself longing for it to be over. It was the strain of it all, watching Ben, watching Amy—who was the centre of everything. Her head was too big, her body too squat, but she was full of love and kisses and everyone adored her. Helen, who had longed to make a pet of Ben, was now able to love Amy. Ben watched all this, silent, and Harriet could not read the look in those cold yellow-green eyes. But then she never could! Sometimes it seemed to her

66

that she spent her life trying to understand what Ben was feeling, thinking. Amy, who expected everyone to love her, would go up to Ben, chuckling, laughing, her arms out. Twice his age, but apparently half his age, this afflicted infant, who was radiant with affection, suddenly became silent; her face was woeful, and she backed away, staring at him. Just like Mr. McGregor, the poor cat. Then she began to cry whenever she saw him. Ben's eyes were never off her, this other afflicted one, adored by everyone in the house. But did he know himself afflicted? Was he, in fact? *What was he?*

Christmas ended, and Ben was two and a few months old. Paul was sent to a little nursery school down the road, to get him away from Ben. The naturally high-spirited and friendly child was becoming nervous and irritable. He had fits of tears or of rage, throwing himself on the floor screaming, or battering at Harriet's knees, trying to get her attention, which never seemed to leave Ben.

Dorothy went off to visit Sarah and her family.

Harriet was alone with Ben during the day. She tried to be with him as she had with the others. She sat on the floor with building blocks and toys you could push about. She showed him colourful pictures. She sang him little rhymes. But Ben did not seem to connect with the toys, or the blocks. He sat among the litter of bright objects and might put one block on another, looking at Harriet to see if this was what he should do. He stared hard at pictures held out to him, trying to decipher their language. He would never sit on Harriet's knees, but squatted by her, and when she said, "That's a bird, Ben, look—just like that bird on that tree. And that's a flower," he stared, and then turned away. Apparently it was not that he could not understand how this block fitted into that or how to make a pile of them, rather that he could not grasp the point of it all, nor of the flower, nor the bird. Perhaps he was too advanced for this sort of game? Sometimes Harriet thought he was. His response to her nursery pictures was that he went out into the garden and stalked a thrush on the lawn, crouching down and moving in a low fast run—and he nearly did catch the thrush. He tore some primroses off their stems, and stood with them in his hands, intently staring at them. Then he crushed them in his strong little fists and let them drop. He turned his head and saw Harriet looking at him: he seemed to be thinking that she wanted him to do something, but what? He stared at the spring flowers, looked up at a blackbird on a branch, and came slowly indoors again.

One day, he talked. Suddenly. He did not say, "Mummy," or "Daddy," or his own name. He said, "I want cake." Harriet did not even notice, at first, that he was talking. Then she did, and told everyone, "Ben's talking. He's using sentences." As their way was, the other children encouraged him: "That's very good, Ben," "Clever Ben!" But he took no notice of them. From then on he announced his needs. "I want that." "Give me that." "Go for a walk now." His voice was heavy and uncertain, each word separate, as if his brain were a lumber-house of ideas and objects, and he had to identify each one.

The children were relieved he was talking normally. "Hello, Ben," one would say. "Hello," Ben replied, carefully handing back exactly what he had been given. "How are you, Ben?" Helen asked. "How are you?" he replied. "No" said Helen, "now you must say, 'I'm very well, thank you,' or, 'I'm fine.' "

Ben stared while he worked it out. Then he said clumsily, "I'm very well."

He watched the children, particularly Luke and Helen, all the time. He studied how they moved, sat down, stood up; copied how they ate. He had understood that these two, the older ones, were more socially accomplished than Jane; and he ignored Paul altogether. When the children watched television, he squatted near them and looked from the screen to their faces, for he needed to know what reactions were appropriate. If they laughed, then, a moment later, he contributed a loud, hard, unnatural-sounding laugh. What was natural to him, it seemed, in the way of amusement was his hostile-looking teeth-bared grin, that looked hostile. When they became silent and still with attention, because of some exciting moment, then he tensed his muscles, like them, and seemed absorbed in the screen— but really he kept his eyes on them.

Altogether, he was easier. Harriet thought: Well, any ordinary child is at its most difficult for about a year after it gets to its feet. No sense of self-preservation, no sense of danger: they hurl themselves off beds and chairs, launch themselves into space, run into roads, have to be watched every second. . . . And they are also, she added, at their most charming, delightful, heart-breakingly sweet and funny. And then they gradually become sensible and life is easier.

Life had become easier . . . but this was only as she saw it, as Dorothy brought home to her.

Dorothy came back to this household after what she called "a rest" of some weeks, and Harriet could see her mother was preparing for a "real talk" with her.

"Now, girl, would you say that I am interfering? That I give you a lot of unwanted advice?"

They were sitting at the big table, mid-morning, with cups of coffee. Ben was where they could watch him, as always. Dorothy was trying to make what she said humorous, but Harriet felt threatened. Her mother's honest pink cheeks were bright with embarrassment, her blue eyes anxious.

"No," said Harriet. "You aren't. You don't."

"Well, now I'm going to have my say."

But she had to stop: Ben began banging a stone against a metal tray. He did this with all his force. The noise was awful, but the women waited until Ben stopped: interrupted, he would have raged and hissed and spat.

"You have five children," Dorothy said. "Not one. Do you

realise that I might just as well be the mother of the others when I'm here? No, I don't believe you do, you've got so taken over by . . ."

Ben again banged the tray with his stone, in a frenzy of exulting accomplishment. It looked as if he believed he was hammering metal, forging something: one could easily imagine him, in the mines deep under the earth, with his kind. . . . Again they waited until he stopped the noise.

"It's not right," said Dorothy. And Harriet remembered how her mother's "That's not right!" had regulated her childhood.

"I'm getting on, you know," said Dorothy. "I can't go on like this, or I'll get ill."

Yes, Dorothy was rather thin, even gaunt. Yes, Harriet thought, full of guilt as usual, she should have noticed.

"And you have a husband, too," said Dorothy, apparently not knowing how she was turning the knife in her daughter's heart. "He's very good, you know, Harriet. I don't know how he puts up with it."

The Christmas after Ben became three only partly filled the house. A cousin of David's had said, "I've been inspired by you, Harriet! After all, I've got a home, too. It's not as big as yours, but it's a nice little house." Several of the family went there. But others said they were coming: made a point of coming, Harriet realised. These were the near relations.

Again a pet was brought. This time it was a big dog, a cheerful boisterous mongrel, Sarah's children's friend, but most particularly Amy's. Of course all the children loved him, but Paul most of all, and this made Harriet's heart ache, for they could have no dog or cat in their home. She even thought: Well, now Ben is more sensible, perhaps . . . But she knew it was impossible. She watched how the big dog seemed to know that Amy, the loving little child in the big ugly body, needed gentleness: he moderated his exuberance for her. Amy would sit by the dog with her arm around his neck, and if she was clumsy with him, he lifted his muzzle and gently pushed her away a little, or gave a small warning sound that said, "Be careful." Sarah said this dog was like a nursemaid to Amy. "Just like Nana in *Peter Pan*," the children said. But if Ben was in the room, the dog watched him carefully and went to lie in a corner, his head on his paws, stiff with attention. One morning when people were sitting around having breakfast, Harriet for some reason turned her head and saw the dog, asleep, and Ben going silently up to him in a low crouch, hands held out in front of him. . . .

"Ben!" said Harriet sharply. She saw those cold eyes turn towards her, caught a gleam of pure malice.

The dog, alerted, scrambled up, and his hair stood on end. He whined anxiously, and came into the part of the room where they all were, and lay down under the table.

Everyone had seen this, and sat silent, while Ben came to Dorothy and said, "I want milk." She poured him some, and he drank it down. Then he looked at them all staring at him. Again he seemed to be trying to understand them. He went into the garden, where they could see him, a squat little gnome, poking with a stick at the earth. The other children were upstairs somewhere.

Around the table sat Dorothy, with Amy on her lap, Sarah, Molly, Frederick, James, and David. Also Angela, the successful sister, "the coper," whose children were all normal.

The atmosphere made Harriet say defiantly, "All right, then, let's have it."

She thought it not without significance, as they say, that it was Frederick who said, "Now look here, Harriet, you've got to face it, he's got to go into an institution."

"Then we have to find a doctor who says he's abnormal," said Harriet. "Dr. Brett certainly won't."

"Get another doctor," said Molly. "These things can be arranged." The two large haystacky people, with their red well-fed faces, were united in determination, nothing vague about them now they had decided there was a crisis, and one that— even indirectly—threatened them. They looked like a pair of judges after a good lunch, Harriet thought, and glanced at David to see if she could share this criticism with him; but he was staring down at the table, mouth tight. He agreed with them.

Angela said, laughing, "Typical upper-class ruthlessness."

No one could remember that note being struck, or at least not so sharply, at this table before. Silence, and then Angela softened it with "Not that I don't agree."

"Of course you agree," said Molly. "Anyone sensible would have to."

"It's the way you said it," said Angela.

"What does it matter how it is said?" enquired Frederick.

"And who is going to pay for it?" asked David. "I can't. All I can do is to keep the bills paid, and that is with James's help."

"Well, James is going to have to bear the brunt of this one," said Frederick, "but we'll chip in." It was the first time this couple had offered any financial help. "Mean, like all their sort," the rest of the family had agreed; and now this judgement was being remembered. They would come for a stay of ten days and contribute a pair of pheasants, a couple of bottles of very good wine. Their "chipping in," everyone knew, wouldn't amount to much.

Full of division, the family sat silent.

Then James said, "I'll do what I can. But things are not as good as they were. Yachts are not everyone's priority in hard times."

Silence again, and everyone was looking at Harriet.

"You are funny people," she said, setting herself apart from them. "You've been here so often and you *know*—I mean, *you* really know what the problem is. What are we going to say to the people who run this institution?"

"It depends on the institution," said Molly, and her large

person seemed full of energy, conviction: as if she had swallowed Ben whole and was digesting him, thought Harriet. She said, mildly enough, though she trembled, "You mean, we have to find one of those places that exist in order to take on children families simply want to get rid of?"

"Rich families," said Angela, with a defiant little sniff.

Molly, confronting impertinence, said firmly, "Yes. If there is no other kind of place. But one thing is obvious: if something isn't done, then it's going to be catastrophic."

"It *is* catastrophic," said Dorothy, firmly taking her position. "The other children . . . they're suffering. You're so involved with it, girl, that you don't see it."

"Look," said David, impatient and angry because he could not stand this, fibres tangled with Harriet, with his parents, being tugged and torn. "Look, I agree. And some time Harriet is going to have to agree. And as far as I am concerned, that time is now. I don't think I can stick it any longer." And now he did look at his wife, and it was a pleading, suffering look. *Please*, he was saying to Harriet. *Please*.

"Very well," said Harriet. "If some place can be found that . . ." And she began to cry.

Ben came in from the garden and stood watching them, in his usual position, which was apart from everyone else. He wore brown dungarees and a brown shirt, both in strong material. Everything he wore had to be thick, because he tore his clothes, destroyed them. With his yellowish stubbly low-growing hair, his stony unblinking eyes, his stoop, his feet planted apart and his knees bent, his clenched held-forward fists, he seemed more than ever like a gnome.

"She is crying," he remarked, of his mother. He took a piece of bread off the table and went out.

"All right," said Harriet, "what *are* you going to tell them?"

"Leave it to us," said Frederick.

"Yes," said Molly.

73

"My God!" said Angela, with a kind of bitter appreciation of them. "Sometimes when I'm with you, I understand everything about this country."

"Thank you," said Molly.

"Thank you," said Frederick.

"You aren't being fair, girl," said Dorothy.

"*Fair*," said Angela, and Harriet, and Sarah, her daughters, almost all at once.

And then everyone but Harriet laughed. In this way was Ben's fate decided.

A few days later, Frederick rang to say that a place had been found and a car was coming for Ben. At once. Tomorrow.

Harriet was frantic: the haste of it, the—yes, ruthlessness! And the doctor who had authorised this? Or would? A doctor who had not even seen Ben? She said all this to David, and knew from his manner that a good deal had gone on behind her back. His parents had talked to him at his office. David had said something like "Yes, I'll see to it" when Molly, whom suddenly Harriet hated, had said, "You'll have to be firm with Harriet."

"It's either him or us," said David to Harriet. He added, his voice full of cold dislike for Ben, "He's probably just dropped in from Mars. He's going back to report on what he's found down here." He laughed—cruelly, it seemed to Harriet, who was silently taking in the fact—which of course she had half known already—that Ben was not expected to live long in this institution, whatever it was.

"He's a little child," she said. "*He's our child.*"

"No, he's not," said David, finally. "Well, he certainly isn't mine."

They were in the living-room. Children's voices rose sharp and distant from the dark winter garden. On the same impulse, David and Harriet went to the window and pulled back the heavy curtains. The garden held dim shapes of tree and shrub, but the light from this warm room reached across the lawn to a shrub that was starkly black with winter, lit twiggy growths that showed a glitter of water, and illuminated the white trunk of a birch. Two small figures, indistinguishably unisex in their many-coloured padded jackets, trousers, woollen caps, emerged from the black under a holly thicket, and came forward. They were Helen and Luke, on some adventure. Both held sticks and were prodding them here and there into last year's leaves.

"Here it is!" Helen's voice rose in triumph, and the parents saw, emerging into the light on the end of the stick, the summer's lost red-and-yellow plastic ball. It was dirtied and squashed, but whole. The two children began a fast stamping dance around and around, the rescued ball held aloft in triumph. Then, suddenly, for no obvious reason, they came racing up to the French doors. The parents sat down on a sofa, facing the doors, which burst inwards, and there they were, two slight, elegant little creatures, with flaring red, frost-burned cheeks and eyes full of the excitements of the dark wilderness they had been part of. They stood breathing heavily, their eyes slowly adjusting to reality, the warm, lit family room and their parents sitting there looking at them. For a moment it was the meeting of two alien forms of life: the children had been part of some old savagery, and their blood still pounded with it; but now they had to let their wild selves go away while they rejoined their family. Harriet and David shared this with them, were with them in imagination and in memory, from their own childhoods: they could see themselves clearly, two adults, sitting there, tame, domestic, even pitiable in their distance from wildness and freedom.

Seeing their parents there alone, no other children around, and above all, no Ben, Helen came to her father, Luke to his mother, and Harriet and David embraced their two adventurous little children, *their* children, holding them tight.

Next morning the car, which was a small black van, came for Ben. Harriet had known it was coming, because David had

75

not gone to work. He had stayed so as to "handle" her! David went upstairs, and brought down suitcases and holdalls that he had packed quietly while she was giving the children breakfast.

He flung these into the van. Then, his face set hard, so that Harriet hardly knew him, he picked Ben up from where he sat on the floor in the living-room, carried him to the van, and put him in. Then he came fast to Harriet, with the same hard set face, and put his arm around her, turned her away from the sight of the van, which was already on its way (she could hear yells and shouts coming from inside it), and took her to the sofa, where—still holding her tight—he said, over and over again, "We have to do it, Harriet. We have to." She was weeping with the shock of it, and with relief, and with gratitude to him, who was taking all the responsibility.

When the children came home, they were told Ben had gone to stay with someone.

"With Granny?" asked Helen, anxious.

"No."

Four pairs of suspicious, apprehensive eyes became suddenly full of relief. Hysterical relief. The children danced about, unable to help themselves, and then pretended it was a game they had thought up then and there.

At supper they were overbright, giggling, hysterical. But in a quiet moment Jane asked shrilly, "Are you going to send us away, too?" She was a stolid, quiet little girl, Dorothy in miniature, never saying anything unnecessary. But now her large blue eyes were fixed in terror on her mother's face.

"No, of course we aren't," said David, sounding curt.

Luke explained, "They are sending Ben away because he isn't really one of us."

In the days that followed, the family expanded like paper flowers in water. Harriet understood what a burden Ben had been, how he had oppressed them all, how much the children had suffered; knew that they had talked about it much more than the parents had wanted to know, had tried to come to terms with Ben. But now Ben was gone their eyes shone, they were full of high spirits, and they kept coming to Harriet with little gifts of a sweet or a toy, "This is for you, Mummy." Or they rushed up to kiss her, or stroke her face, or nuzzle to her like happy calves or foals. And David took days off from work to be with them all—to be with her. He was careful with her, tender. As if I were ill, she decided rebelliously. Of course she thought all the time of Ben, who was a prisoner somewhere. What kind of a prisoner? She pictured the little black van, remembered his cries of rage as he was taken away.

The days went by, and normality filled the house. Harriet heard the children talking about the Easter holidays. "It will be all right now that Ben isn't here," said Helen.

They had always understood so much more than she had wanted to acknowledge.

While she was part of the general relief, and could hardly believe she had been able to stand such strain, and for so long, she could not banish Ben from her mind. It was not with love, or even affection, that she thought of him, and she disliked herself for not being able to find one little spark of normal feeling: it was guilt and horror that kept her awake through the nights. David knew she was awake, though she did try to hide it.

Then one morning she started up out of sleep, out of a bad dream, though she did not know what, and she said, "I'm going to see what they are doing to Ben."

David opened his eyes, and lay silent, staring over his arm at the window. He had been dozing, not asleep. She knew he had feared this, and there was something about him then that said to her: Right, then that's it, it's enough.

"David, I've got to."

"Don't," he said.

"I simply have to."

77

Again she knew from the way he lay there, not looking at her, and did not say anything more than that one syllable, that it was bad for her, that he was making decisions as he lay there. He stayed where he was for a few minutes, and then got out of bed, and went out of the room and downstairs.

When she had got her clothes on, she rang Molly, who was at once coldly angry. "No, I'm not going to tell you where it is. Now you've done it, then leave it alone."

But at last she did give Harriet the address.

Again Harriet was wondering why she was always treated like a criminal. Ever since Ben was born it's been like this, she thought. Now it seemed to her the truth, that everyone had silently condemned her. I have suffered a misfortune, she told herself; I haven't committed a crime.

Ben had been taken to a place in the North of England; it would be four or five hours' drive—perhaps more, if she was unlucky with the traffic. There was bad traffic, and she drove through grey wintry rain. It was early afternoon when she approached a large solid building of dark stone, in a valley high among moors she could hardly see for grey drifting rain. The place stood square and upright among dismal dripping evergreens, and its regular windows, three rows of them, were barred.

She entered a small entrance lobby that had a handwritten card tacked on the inner door: "Ring for Attendance." She rang, and waited, and nothing happened. Her heart was beating. She still surged with the adrenaline that had given her the impetus to come, but the long drive had subdued her, and this oppressive building was telling her nerves, if not her intelligence—for, after all, she had no facts to go on—that what she had feared was true. Yet she did not know exactly what that was. She rang again. The building was silent: she could hear the shrill of a bell a long way off in its interior. Again, nothing, and she was about to go around to the back when the door abruptly opened to show a slatternly girl wearing jerseys, cardigans, and a thick scarf. She had a pale little face under a mass of curly yellow hair that had a blue ribbon holding a queue like a sheep's tail. She seemed tired.

"Yes?" she asked.

Harriet saw, understanding what this meant, that people simply did not come here.

She said, already stubborn, "I'm Mrs. Lovatt and I've come to see my son."

It was evident that these were words this institution, whatever it was, did not expect to meet.

The girl stared, gave an involuntary little shake of the head that expressed incapacity, and then said, "Dr. MacPherson isn't here this week." She was Scottish, too, and her accent was strong.

"Someone must be deputising for him," said Harriet decisively.

The girl fell back before Harriet's manner, smiling uncertainly, and very worried. She muttered, "Wait here, then," and went inside. Harriet followed her before the big door was shut to exclude her. The girl did glance around, as if she planned to say, You must wait outside, but instead she said, "I'll fetch someone," and went on into the dark caverns of a corridor that had small ceiling lights all along it, hardly disturbing the gloom. There was a smell of disinfectant. Absolute silence. No, after a time Harriet became aware of a high thin screaming that began, and stopped, and went on again, coming from the back of the building.

Nothing happened. Harriet went out into the vestibule, which was already darkening with the approaching night. The rain was now a cold deluge, silent and regular. The moors had disappeared.

She rang again, decisively, and returned to the corridor.

Two figures appeared, a long way off under the pinpoints of

the ceiling lights, and came towards her. A young man, in a white coat that was not clean, was followed by the girl, who now had a cigarette in her mouth and was screwing up her eyes from the smoke. Both looked tired and uncertain.

He was an ordinary young man, though worn down in a general way; taken bit by bit, hands, face, eyes, he was unremarkable, but there was something desperate about him, as if he contained anger, or hopelessness.

"You can't be here," he said, in a flurried indecisive way. "We don't have visiting days here." His voice was South London, flat and nasal.

"But I am here," said Harriet. "I am here to see my son Ben Lovatt."

And suddenly he took in a breath, and looked at the girl, who pursed her lips together and raised her eyebrows.

"Listen," said Harriet. "I don't think you understand. I'm not just going away, you know. I've come to see my son, and that is what I am going to do."

He knew she meant it. He slowly nodded, as if saying, Yes, but that isn't the point. He was looking hard at her. She was being given a warning, and from someone who was taking the responsibility for it. He might be a rather pitiable young man, and certainly an overtired and inadequately fed one, doing this job because he could not get another, but the weight of his position—the unhappy weight of it—was speaking through him, and his expression and his reddened, smoke-tired eyes were severe, authoritative, to be taken seriously.

"When people dump their kids here, they don't come and see them after," he said.

"You see, you don't understand at all," said the girl.

Harriet heard herself explode with "I'm sick of being told I don't understand this and that. I'm the child's mother. I'm Ben Lovatt's mother. Do *you* understand that?"

Suddenly they were all three together in understanding, even in desperate acceptance of some kind of general fatality.

He nodded, and said, "Well, I'll go and see . . . "

"And I am coming, too," she said.

This really did alert him. "Oh no," he exclaimed, "you are *not!*" He said something to the girl, who began running surprisingly fast down the corridor. "You stay here," he said to Harriet, and strode after the girl.

Harriet saw the girl turn right and disappear, and without thinking she opened a door at her right hand. She saw the young man's arm raised in imprecation, or warning, while what was behind that door reached her.

She was at the end of a long ward, which had any number of cots and beds along the walls. In the cots were—monsters. While she strode rapidly through the ward to the door at the other end, she was able to see that every bed or cot held an infant or small child in whom the human template had been wrenched out of pattern, sometimes horribly, sometimes slightly. A baby like a comma, great lolling head on a stalk of a body . . . then something like a stick insect, enormous bulging eyes among stiff fragilities that were limbs . . . a small girl all blurred, her flesh guttering and melting . . . a doll with chalky swollen limbs, its eyes wide and blank, like blue ponds, and its mouth open, showing a swollen little tongue. A lanky boy was skewed, one half of his body sliding from the other. A child seemed at first glance normal, but then Harriet saw there was no back to its head; it was all face, which seemed to scream at her. Rows of freaks, nearly all asleep, and all silent. They were literally drugged out of their minds. Well, nearly silent: there was a dreary sobbing from a cot that had its sides shielded with blankets. The high intermittent screaming, nearer now, still assaulted her nerves. A smell of excrement, stronger than the disinfectant. Then she was out of the nightmare ward and in another corridor, parallel to the one she had first seen, and identical. At its end she saw the girl, followed by the young man, come a little way towards her and then again turn right. . . . Harriet ran fast, hearing her feet thud on the boards, and turned where they did, and was in a tiny room holding trolleys of medicines and drugs. She ran through this and was now in a long cement-floored passage that had doors with inspection grilles in them all along the wall facing her. The young man and the girl were opening one of these doors as she arrived beside them. All three were breathing heavily.

"Shit," said the young man, meaning her being there.

"Literally," said Harriet as the door opened on a square room whose walls were of white shiny plastic that was buttoned here and there and looked like fake expensive leather upholstery. On the floor, on a green foam-rubber mattress, lay Ben. He was unconscious. He was naked, inside a strait-jacket. His pale yellow tongue protruded from his mouth. His flesh was dead white, greenish. Everything—walls, the floor, and Ben—was smeared with excrement. A pool of dark yellow urine oozed from the pallet, which was soaked.

"I told you not to come!" shouted the young man. He took Ben's shoulders and the girl Ben's feet. From the way they touched the child, Harriet saw they were not brutal; that was not the point at all. They lifted Ben thus—for in this way they had to touch very little of him—out of this room, along the corridor a little way, and through another door. She followed, and stood watching. This was a room that had sinks all along one wall, an immense bath, and a sloping cement shelf with plugs all along it. They put Ben on this shelf, unwound the strait-jacket, and, having adjusted the temperature of the water, began washing him down with a hose that was attached to one of the taps. Harriet leaned against the wall, watching. She was shocked to the point where she felt nothing at all. Ben did not move. He lay like a drowned fish on the slab, was turned over several times by the girl, when the young man interrupted the hosing process for the purpose, and was finally carried by them both to another slab, where they dried him and then took a clean strait-jacket from a pile and put it on him.

"Why?" demanded Harriet, fierce. They did not answer.

They took the child, trussed, unconscious, his tongue lolling, out of the room, down the corridor, and into another room that had a cement shelf like a bed in it. They put Ben on it, and then both stood up and sighed: "Phew."

"Well, there he is," said the young man. He stood for a moment, eyes closed, recovering from the ordeal, and then lit a cigarette. The girl put out her hand for one; he gave it to her. They stood smoking, looking at Harriet in an exhausted, defeated way.

She did not know what to say. Her heart was hurting as it would for one of her own, real children, for Ben looked more ordinary than she had ever seen him, with those hard cold alien eyes of his closed. Pathetic: she had never seen him as pathetic before.

"I think I'll take him home," she said.

"It's up to you," said the young man shortly.

The girl was looking curiously at Harriet, as if she were part of the phenomenon that was Ben, of the same nature. She asked, "What are you going to do with him?" She added, and Harriet recognised fear in her voice, "He's so strong—I've never seen anything like it."

"None of us have seen anything like it," said the young man.

"Where are his clothes?"

Now he laughed, scornful, and said, "You're going to put his clothes on and take him home, just like that?"

"Why not? He was wearing clothes when he came."

The two attendants—nurses, orderlies, whatever they were—

exchanged looks. Then both took a drag on their cigarettes.

He said, "I don't think you understand, Mrs. Lovatt. How far have you got to go, for a start?"

"Four or five hours' driving."

He laughed again, at the impossibility of it—of *her*, Harriet—and said, "He's going to come round on the journey, and then what?"

"Well, he'll see me," she said, and saw from their faces that she was being stupid. "All right, then, what do you advise?"

"Wrap him in a couple of blankets, over the strait-jacket," said the girl.

"And then drive like hell," he said.

The three now stood in silence, looking at each other, a long, sober look.

"You try doing this job," said the girl suddenly, full of rage against fate. "You just try it. Well, I'm leaving at the end of this month."

"And so am I, no one sticks it longer than a few weeks," said the man.

"All right," said Harriet. "I'm not going to complain, or anything."

"You'll have to sign a form. We have to be covered," he said.

But they could not easily find the form. At last, after a lot of rummaging about in a filing cabinet, they produced a slip of paper, mimeographed years ago, that said Harriet acquitted the institution of all responsibility.

Now she picked Ben up, touching him for the first time. He was deadly cold. He lay heavy in her arms, and she understood the words "a dead weight."

She went out into the corridor, saying, "I'm not going through that ward again."

"Who could blame you?" said the young man, wearily sarcastic. He had got hold of a load of blankets, and they wrapped Ben in two, carried him out to the car, laid him on the back seat, and piled more blankets over him. Only his face showed.

She stood with the two young people by the car. They could hardly see each other. Apart from the car lights, and the lights of the building, it was dark. Water squelched under foot. The young man took out of his overall pocket a plastic package containing a syringe, a couple of needles, and some ampules.

"You had better take these," he said.

Harriet hesitated, and the girl said, "Mrs. Lovatt, I don't think you realise—"

She nodded, took the package, got in.

"You can give him up to four shots a day, not more," said the young man.

As she was about to let the clutch pedal out, she asked, "Tell me, how long do you think he would have lasted?"

Their faces were white patches in the gloom, but she could see that he shook his head, turning away. The girl's voice came: "None of them last long. But this one . . . he's very strong. He's the strongest any of us have seen."

"Which means he would have lasted longer?"

"No," he said. "No, that's not it at all. Because he's so strong, he fights all the time, and so he has to have bigger shots. It kills them."

"All right," said Harriet. "Well, thank you both."

They stood watching as she drove off, but almost at once vanished into the wet dark. As she rounded the drive, she saw them standing in the dimly lit porch, close together, as if reluctant to go in.

She drove as fast as she could through the wintry rain, avoiding the main roads, keeping an eye on the heap of blankets behind her. About half-way home she saw the blankets heave and convulse, and Ben woke with a bellow of rage, and thrashed about, landing on the floor of the car, where he began to scream, not like the thin high automatic screaming she had heard at the institution but screams of fear that vibrated through her.

85

She stuck it out for half an hour, feeling the thuds that Ben made vibrate through the car. She was looking for a lay-by that had no other car in it, and when she found one, she stopped, let the engine run, and took out the syringe. She knew how to use it, from some illness of the other children. She broke open the capsule, which had no brand name on it, and filled the syringe. Then she leaned over the back of the seat. Ben, naked except for the strait-jacket, and blue with cold, was heaving and struggling and bellowing. His eyes looked up at her in a glare of hate. He didn't recognise her, she thought. She did not dare unwind the jacket. She was afraid of injecting him anywhere near his neck. At last she managed to grab, and hold, an ankle, jabbed the needle into the lower part of his calf, and waited until he went limp: it took a few moments. What was this stuff?

Again she put him on the back seat under the blankets, and now she drove on the main roads home. She got there at about eight. The children would be sitting around the kitchen table. And David would be with them: he would not have gone to work.

With Ben a mound of blankets in her arms, his face covered, she went into the living-room, and looked over the low wall to where they all sat around the big table. Luke. Helen. Jane. Little Paul. And David, his face set and angry. And very tired.

She remarked, "They were killing him," and saw that David would not forgive her for saying this in front of the children. All showed fear.

She went straight up the stairs to the big bedroom, and through it to "the baby's room," and put Ben on the bed. He was waking up. And then it began, the fighting, the heaving, the screaming. Again he was on the floor, rolling around on it; and again he flexed and bent and thrashed, and his eyes were pure hate.

She could not take off the strait-jacket.

She went down into the kitchen, and got milk and biscuits while her family sat and watched her in total silence.

Ben's screams and struggling were shaking the house.

"The police will be here," said David.

"Keep them quiet," she commanded, and went up with the food.

When Ben saw what she held, he became silent and still, and his eyes were avid. She lifted him like a mummy, put the cup of milk to his lips, and he almost drowned as he gulped: he was starving. She fed him bits of biscuit, keeping her fingers clear of his teeth. When what she had brought was finished, he began roaring and flailing again. She gave him another jab.

The children were in front of the television, but were not watching it. Jane and Paul were crying. David sat at the table with his head in his hands. She said softly, for him to hear, "All right, I am a criminal. But they were murdering him."

He did not move. She had her back to him. She did not want to see his face.

She said, "He would have been dead in a few months. Weeks, probably." A silence. At last she turned. She could hardly bear to look at him. He looked ill, but that was not it. . . .

She said, "I couldn't stand it."

He said deliberately, "I thought that was the idea."

She cried out, "Yes, but you didn't see it, you didn't see—!"

"I was careful *not* to see," he said. "What did you suppose was going to happen? That they were going to turn him into some well-adjusted member of society and then everything would be lovely?" He was jeering at her, but it was because his throat was stiff with tears.

Now they looked at each other, long, hard, seeing everything about each other. She thought, All right, he was right, and I was wrong. But it's done.

She said aloud, "All right, but it's done."

"That's the *mot juste*, I think."

She sat down beside the children on the sofa. Now she saw

they all had tear-stained faces. She could not touch them to comfort them, because it was she who made them cry.

When she at last said "Bed," they all got up at once and went, without looking at her.

She took supplies of suitable food for Ben up to the big bedroom. David had moved his things to another room.

When Ben woke towards morning and began his roaring, she fed him, and drugged him.

She gave the children breakfast as always, and tried to be normal. They tried, too. No one mentioned Ben.

When David came down, she said, "Please take them to school."

Then the house had only her and Ben in it. When he woke, she fed him but did not drug him. He roared and struggled, but, she thought, much less.

In a lull, when he seemed worn out, she said, "Ben, you are at home, not in that place." He was listening.

"When you stop making all that noise, I'll take you out of that thing they put you in."

It was too soon, he began struggling again. Through his screams she heard voices, and went to the banisters. David had not gone to his office, had stayed home to help her. Two young policewomen stood there, and David was talking to them. They went away.

What had they been told? She did not ask.

Towards the time the children were due home, she said to Ben, "I want you to be quiet now, Ben. The other children will be here and you'll frighten them screaming like that."

He became quiet: it was exhaustion.

He was on the floor, which was by now streaked with excrement. She carried him to the bathroom, took off the jacket, put him in the bath and washed him, and saw that he was shuddering with terror: he had not always been unconscious when they washed him in that place. She took him back to the bed, and said, "If you start all that again, then I'm going to have to put that thing back on you."

He ground his teeth at her, his eyes blazing. But he was afraid, too. She was going to have to control him through fear.

She cleaned his room while he lay moving his arms about, as if he had forgotten how to do it. He had been in that cloth prison, probably, ever since he had been in the institution.

Then he squatted on his bed, moving his arms and staring around his room, recognising it, and her, at last.

He said, "Open the door."

She said, "No, not until I am sure you will behave well."

He was about to start again, but she shouted at him, "Ben, I mean it! You shout and scream and I'll tie you up."

He controlled himself. She handed him sandwiches, which he crammed into his mouth, choking.

He had unlearned all the basic social skills that it had been so hard to teach him.

She talked quietly while he ate. "And now listen to me, Ben. You have to listen. You behave well and everything will be all right. You must eat properly. You must use the pot or go to the lavatory. And you mustn't scream and fight." She was not sure he heard her. She repeated it. She went on repeating it.

That evening she stayed with Ben, and she did not see the other children at all. David went up to the other room away from her. How she felt at this time was that she was shielding them from Ben while she re-educated him for family life. But how they felt it, she knew, was that she had turned her back on them all and chosen to go off into alien country, with Ben.

That night she locked the door on him, and bolted it, left him undrugged and hoped he would sleep. He did, but woke, screaming in fear. She went in to him, and found him backed against the wall at the end of the bed, an arm up over his face, unable to hear her, while she talked, and talked, using reasonable persuasive words against this storm of terror. At last he became quiet and she gave him food. He could not get enough food: he had really been starving. They had had to keep him drugged, and, when drugged, he could not eat.

Fed, he again backed himself against the wall, squatted on the bed, and looked at the door where his jailers would enter: he had not really understood he was at home.

Then he nodded off . . . woke with a bellow; nodded off . . . woke . . . She calmed him, and he dropped off.

Days passed; nights passed.

He at last understood he was at home and safe. Slowly, he stopped eating as if every mouthful were his last. Slowly, he used his pot, and then allowed himself to be taken by the hand along the passage to the lavatory. Then he came downstairs, darting glances around him to see the enemy before he could be captured again. As he saw it, this house was where he had been trapped. And by his father. When he first set eyes on David, he backed away, hissing.

David did not try to reassure him; as far as he was concerned, Ben was Harriet's responsibility, and his was for the children—the real children.

Ben took his place at the big table, among the other children. He kept his eyes on his father, who had betrayed him. Helen said, "Hello, Ben." Then Luke: "Hello, Ben." Then Jane. Not Paul, who was miserable that Ben was there again, and took himself off to flump into a chair and pretend to watch television.

Ben at last said, "Hello." His eyes were moving from face to face: friend or foe?

He ate, watching them. When they went to sit and watch television, he did, too, copying them for safety, and looked at the screen because they did.

And so things went back to normal, if that was a word that could be used.

But Ben did not trust his father; he never trusted him again.

David could not even come near him without Ben freezing, and backing away, and, if he came too close, snarling.

When she was sure Ben had recovered, Harriet acted on an idea she had been developing. The garden had got badly out of hand last summer, and a youth called John came to help with it. He was unemployed, and did odd jobs.

For a few days he had cut hedges, dug up a couple of ailing shrubs, sawed off a dead branch, mowed the lawn. Ben would not be parted from him. He crouched at the French doors, waiting for John to arrive; then followed him around like a puppy. John did not mind Ben at all. He was a big, shaggy, amiable youth, good-natured, patient: he treated Ben in a rough-and-ready way, as if Ben were indeed a puppy that needed training. "No, you must sit there now and wait till I've done." "Hold these shears for me, that's right." "No, I'm going home now, you can come to the gate with me."

Ben sometimes whined and grizzled when John went off.

Now Harriet went down to a certain café—"Betty's Caff," as it was known—where she knew he hung out, and found him there with some mates. This was a gang of unemployed young men, about ten of them, and sometimes there were a couple of girls. She did not bother to explain anything, for by now she knew that people understood very well—that is, if they weren't experts, doctors.

She sat among these youths, and said that it would be two years, perhaps more, before Ben went to school. He wasn't suitable for ordinary nursery school. She looked at John deliberately, in the eyes, when she used the word "suitable," and he simply nodded. She would like Ben taken care of during the day. The money would be good.

"You want me up at your house?" John asked, saying no to this proposition.

"It would be up to you," said Harriet. "He likes you, John. He trusts you."

He looked at his mates: they consulted each other with their eyes. Then he nodded.

Now he arrived most mornings about nine, and Ben went off with him on his motorbike: went exultantly, laughing, without a look back at his mother, his father, his brothers and sisters. The understanding was that Ben should be kept well away from his home until supper time, but often it was long after that when he arrived. He had become part of the group of young unemployed, who hung about on pavements, sat around in cafés, sometimes did odd jobs, went to the cinema, rushed about on motorbikes or in borrowed cars.

The family became a family again. Well, almost.

David came back to sleep in the connubial room. There was a distance between them. David had made and now kept this distance because Harriet had hurt him so badly: she understood this. Harriet informed him that she was now on the Pill: for both it was a bleak moment, because of everything they had been, had stood for, in the past, which had made it impossible for her to be on the Pill. They had felt it deeply wrong so to tamper with the processes of Nature! Nature—they now reminded themselves they once felt—was at some level or other to be relied upon.

Harriet rang up Dorothy and asked her if she would come for a week, and then begged David to go off with her on a holiday somewhere. They had not been alone, ever, since Luke was born. They chose a quiet country hotel, and walked a good deal, and were considerate with each other. Their hearts ached a good deal; but then that seemed to be something they must live with. Sometimes, particularly in their happiest moments, they could not stop their eyes from filling. But at nights when she lay in her husband's arms, Harriet knew this was nothing like the real thing, not like the past.

She said, "Suppose we do what we said we would—I mean, go on having children?"

She felt how his body tensed, felt his anger.

"And so it all never happened?" he asked at last, and she knew he was curious to hear her: he could not believe his ears!

"Another Ben wouldn't happen again—why should it?"

"It's not a question of another Ben," he remarked at last, and he was keeping his voice emotionless because of his anger.

She knew that what he could have assaulted her with was exactly what she always tried to conceal from herself, or at least the worst of it: she had dealt the family a mortal wound when she rescued Ben.

She persisted, "We could have more children."

"And the four we have don't count?"

"Perhaps it would bring us all together again, make things better. . . ."

He was silent; and against that silence she could hear how false her words had rung.

At last he enquired, in the same emotionless way, "And what about Paul?" For it was Paul who was the most damaged.

"Perhaps he would get over it," she said hopelessly.

"He is not going to get over it, Harriet." And now his voice vibrated with what he was suppressing.

She turned away from him, and lay weeping.

When the summer holidays were due, Harriet wrote careful letters to everyone, explaining that Ben was hardly ever in the house. She felt unfaithful and treacherous doing this: but to whom?

Some of them came. Not Molly, or Frederick, who did not forgive her for bringing Ben back; nor would they ever, she knew. Her sister Sarah came with Amy and with Dorothy, who now was Amy's support against the world. But Amy's brothers and sisters went to stay with their other cousins, Angela's children, and the Lovatt children knew they would not have company for the holidays because of Ben. Briefly, Deborah was there. She had been married and divorced since they had seen her. She was a spiky, elegant, increasingly witty and desperate girl, who was a good aunt to the children, in an impulsive unskilled way, with expensive and unsuitable presents. James was there. He said several times that the house was like a large fruit-cake, but this was kindness. There were some grown-up cousins, at a loose end, and a colleague of David's.

And where was Ben? One day, Harriet was shopping in the town, and she heard the roar of a motorbike behind her, and turned to see a creature like a space-age jockey, presumably John, crouched low over the bars, and behind him, clutching tight, a dwarf child: she saw her son Ben, his mouth open in what seemed to be a chant or yell of exultation. Ecstatic. She had never seen him like this. Happy? Was that the word?

She knew he had become a pet or a mascot for this group of young men. They treated him roughly, it seemed to Harriet, even unkindly, calling him Dopey, Dwarfey, Alien Two, Hobbit, and Gremlin. "Hey, Dopey, you're in my way." "Go and fetch me a cigarette from Jack, Hobbit." But he was happy. In the mornings, he was at the window waiting for one of them to come and fetch him; if they failed him, rang up to say they couldn't make it that day, he was full of rage and deprivation, and stamped bellowing about the house.

It was all costing a good bit of money. John and his gang were having good times at the Lovatts' expense. Not only, these days, at the expense of James, Ben's grandfather, for David was doing all kinds of extra work. They did not scruple to put the screws on. "We'll take Ben off to the sea, if you like." "Oh good, that'd be lovely." "It'll be twenty quid, then—there's petrol." And the roaring machines went off to the coast, crowded with young men and girls, Ben with them. When they returned him: "That cost more than we thought." "How much?" "Another ten quid."

"It's very nice for him," a cousin might say, hearing that Ben was off to the seaside—just as if this were a normal thing, a little boy being taken off for a treat.

He would come in from a day of safety and enjoyment with John and his mates, where he was teased and roughed up, but accepted, and stand by the table, where his family was, all looking at him, their faces grave and cautious. "Give me bread," he would say. "Give me biscuits."

"Sit down, Ben," Luke, or Helen, or Jane—never Paul— would say, in the patient, decent way they had with him, which hurt Harriet.

He scrambled energetically onto a chair, and set himself to be like them. He knew he mustn't talk with his mouth full, for instance, or eat with his mouth open. He carefully obeyed such imperatives, the energetic animal movements of his jaws confined behind closed lips, waiting till his mouth was empty before saying, "Ben get down now. Ben wants go to bed."

He was not in "the baby's room" now, but the one nearest to his parents on the landing. (The baby's room was empty.) They could not lock him in at night: the sound of a key turning, the slide of a bolt, made him explode into screaming, kicking rage. But the last thing before they slept, the other children locked their doors quietly from inside. This meant Harriet could not go in to them to see how they were before she went to bed, or if they were sick. She did not like to ask them not to lock their doors, nor make a big thing of it by calling in a locksmith and having special locks fitted, openable from the outside by an adult with a key. This business of the children locking themselves in made her feel excluded, forever shut out and repudiated by them. Sometimes she went softly to one of their doors and whispered to be let in, and she was admitted, and there was a little festival of kisses and hugs—but they were thinking of Ben, who might come in . . . and several times he did arrive silently in the doorway and stare in at this scene, which he could not understand.

Harriet would have liked to lock their door. David said, trying to joke about it, that he would, one of these days. More than once she woke to see Ben standing silently there in the half dark, staring at them. The shadows from the garden moved on the ceiling, the spaces of the big room emptied into obscurity, and there stood this goblin child, half visible. The pressure of those inhuman eyes of his had entered her sleep and woken her.

"Go to sleep, Ben," she would say gently, keeping her voice level because of the sharp fear she felt. What was he thinking as he stood there, watching them sleep? Did he want to hurt them? Was he experiencing a misery she could not begin to imagine, because he was forever shut out from the ordinariness of this house and its people? Did he want to put his arms around her, like the other children, but not know how? But when she put her arms around him, there was no response, no warmth; it was as if he did not feel her touch.

But, after all, he was in the house very little.

"We aren't far off being normal again," she said to David. Hopefully. Longing for him to reassure her. But he only nodded, and did not look at her.

In fact, those two years before Ben went to school were not too bad: afterwards she looked back on them gratefully.

In the year Ben was five, Luke and Helen announced they wanted to go to boarding-school. They were thirteen and eleven. Of course this went against everything Harriet and David believed in. They said this; said, too, that they could not afford it. But again the parents had to face how much the children understood, how they discussed, and planned—and then acted. Luke had already written to Grandfather James, Helen to Grandmother Molly. Their fees would be paid for.

Luke said, in his reasonable way, "They agree it would be better for us. We know you can't help it, but we don't like Ben."

This had happened just after Harriet had come down one morning, Luke and Helen, Jane and Paul behind her, to see Ben squatting on the big table, with an uncooked chicken he had taken from the refrigerator, which stood open, its contents spilled all over the floor. Ben had raided it in some savage fit he could not control. Grunting with satisfaction, he tore the raw chicken apart with teeth and hands, pulsing with barbaric strength. He had looked up over the partly shredded and dismembered carcass at Harriet, at his siblings, and snarled. Then Harriet saw the vitality die down in him as she scolded, "*Naughty* Ben," and he made himself stand up there on the table, and then jump down to the floor and face her, the remains of the chicken dangling in one hand.

"Poor Ben hungry," he whined.

He had taken to calling himself Poor Ben. He had heard someone say this? In the group of young men and their girls, had someone said, "Poor Ben!"—and he had then known it fitted him? Was this how he thought of himself? If so, this was a window into a Ben concealed from them, and it broke one's heart—broke Harriet's heart, to be accurate.

The children had not commented at all on this scene. They had sat themselves around the table for breakfast, looking at each other, not at her or at Ben.

There was no way Ben could get out of going to school. She had given up trying to read to him, play with him, teach him anything: he could not learn. But she knew the Authorities would never recognise this, or acknowledge that they did. They would say, and rightly, that he did know a lot of things that made him into a part-social being. He knew facts. "Traffic lights green—go. Traffic lights red—stop." Or, "Half a plate of chips, half price big plate of chips." Or, "Shut the door, because it is cold." He would singsong these truths, imparted to him presumably by John, looking at Harriet for confirmation. "Eat with a spoon, not with fingers!" "Hold on tight going around corners." Sometimes Harriet heard him singing these slogans in bed at night, thinking of the delights of the day to come.

When he was told he must go to school, he said he would not. Harriet said there was no way around it, to school he must go. But he could be with John at weekends, and on holidays. Tantrums. Rages. Despair. Roars of "No! No! No!" The whole house resounded with it.

John was summoned; he arrived in the kitchen with three of his gang. John, instructed by Harriet, said to Ben, "Now listen, mate. You just listen to us. You've got to go to school."

"Will you be there?" asked Ben, standing by John's knee, looking trustfully up at him. Rather, his pose, the set of his lifted face, said he trusted John, but his eyes seemed to have shrunk into his head with fear.

"No. But I was at school. When I had to be." Here the four young men laughed, for of course they had played truant, as all their sort did. School was irrelevant to them. "I was at school. Rowland here was at school. Barry and Henry were at school."

"That's right, that's right," they all said, playing their parts.

"And I was at school," said Harriet. But Ben did not hear her: she did not count.

It was finally arranged that Harriet would take Ben to school in the mornings, and that John would be responsible for picking him up. Ben would spend the hours between school's end and bedtime with the gang.

For the sake of the family, thought Harriet; for the children's sake . . . for my sake and David's. Though he seems to come home later and later.

Meanwhile the family had—as she felt it, saw it—fallen apart. Luke and Helen had gone to their respective boarding-schools. In the house were left Jane and Paul, who were both at the same school Ben was at, but being in higher classes would not see much of Ben. Jane continued solid, sensible, quiet, and as able to save herself as Luke or Helen. She seldom came home after school, but went to friends. Paul did come home. He was alone with Harriet, and this, she thought, was what he wanted, and needed. He was demanding, shrill, difficult, often in tears. Where was that enchanting, delicious little child, her Paul, she wondered as he nagged and whined, now a lanky six-year-old, with great soft blue eyes that often stared at nothing, or seemed to protest at what he saw. He was too thin. He had never eaten properly. She brought him home from school and tried to make him sit down and eat, or she sat with him, and read, and told him stories. He could not concentrate. He mooned restlessly about, and daydreamed; then came to Harriet to touch her, or climb on her lap like a smaller child, never appeased or at rest or content.

He had not had a mother at the proper time, and that was the trouble, and they all knew it.

When he heard the roar of the machine that was bringing Ben back home, Paul might burst into tears, or bang his head on the wall with frustration.

After Ben had been at school for a month, and there had been no unpleasant news, she asked his teacher how he was getting on. She heard, to her surprise, "He's a good little chap. He tries so hard."

Towards the end of the first term, she was summoned on the telephone by the headmistress, Mrs. Graves. "Mrs. Lovatt, I wonder if you . . . "

An efficient woman, she knew what went on in her school, and that Harriet was the responsible parent of Luke, Helen, Jane, and Paul.

"We all find ourselves at a loss," said she. "Ben is really trying very hard. He doesn't seem to fit in with the others. It's hard to put one's finger on it."

Harriet sat waiting—as she had done, it seemed to her, far too often in Ben's short life—for some kind of acknowledgement that here might be more than a difficulty of adjustment.

She remarked, "He has always been an oddball."

"The odd man out in the family? Well, there's usually one, I've often noticed it," said affable Mrs. Graves. While this surface conversation went on, the sensitised Harriet was listening for the other, parallel conversation that Ben's existence compelled.

"These young men who come and collect Ben, it's an unusual arrangement," smiled Mrs. Graves.

"He's an unusual child," said Harriet, looking hard at the headmistress, who nodded, not looking at Harriet. She was frowning, as if some annoying thought were poking at her, wanting attention, but she did not feel inclined to give it any.

"Have you ever known a child like Ben before?" Harriet asked.

This risked the headmistress saying, "What do you mean, Mrs. Lovatt?" And in fact Mrs. Graves did say, "What do you mean, Mrs. Lovatt?" but quickly, and then, to stop Harriet telling her, she funked it with "He is hyperactive, perhaps? Of course that is a word that I often feel evades the issue. To say a child is hyperactive does not say very much! But he does have this extraordinary energy. He can't keep still long—well, a lot of children can't. His teacher has found him a rewarding little boy because he does try, but she says she has to put more effort into him than all the rest put together. . . . Well, Mrs. Lovatt, I'm glad you came in, it has been a help." And as Harriet left, she saw how the headmistress watched her, with that long, troubled inspection that held unacknowledged unease, even horror, which was part of "the other conversation"—the real one.

Towards the end of the second term, she was telephoned: Would she come in at once, please? Ben had hurt someone.

Here it was: this is what she had dreaded. Ben had suddenly

gone berserk and attacked a bigger girl in the playground. He had pulled her down, so that she fell heavily on the asphalt, bruising and grazing her legs. Then he had bitten her, and bent back her arm until it broke.

"I have spoken to Ben," said Mrs. Graves. "He doesn't seem to be remorseful in any way. You might even think he doesn't know he did it. But at that age—he is six, after all—he should know what he is doing."

Harriet took Ben home, leaving Paul to be picked up later. It was Paul she wanted to take with her: the child had heard of the attack, and was hysterical, screaming that Ben would kill him, too. But she had to be alone with Ben.

Ben sat on the kitchen table, swinging his legs, eating bread and jam. He had asked if John would come here to pick him up. It was John he needed.

Harriet said, "You hurt poor Mary Jones today. Why did you do that, Ben?"

He seemed not to hear, but tore lumps of bread off with his teeth, and then gulped them down.

Harriet sat down close to him, so that he could not ignore her, and said, "Ben, do you remember that place you went to in the van?"

He went rigid. He slowly turned his head and looked at her. The bread in his hand was trembling: he was trembling. He remembered, all right! She had never done this before—had hoped she would never have to.

"Well, *do* you remember, Ben?"

His eyes had a wild look; he could have jumped down from the table and run off. He wanted to, but was glaring around into the corners of the room, at the windows, up the staircase, as if he might be attacked from these places.

"Now listen to me, Ben. If you ever, ever, *ever* hurt anyone again, you'll have to go back there."

She kept her eyes on his, and hoped that he could not know

she was saying inwardly, But I'd never send him back, never.

He sat shivering, like a wet, cold dog, in spasms, and he went through a series of movements, unconsciously, the vestiges of reactions from that time. A hand went up to shield his face, and he looked through the spread fingers as if this hand could protect him; then the hand fell, and he turned his head away sharply, pressing the back of the other hand to his mouth, glaring in terror over it; he briefly bared his teeth to snarl—but then checked himself; he lifted his chin, and his mouth opened, and Harriet saw that he could have emitted a long, animal howl. It was as if she actually heard this howl, its lonely terror. . . .

"Did you hear me, Ben?" Harriet said softly.

He slid down off the table, and thumped his way up the stairs. He left behind him a thin trail of urine. She heard his door shut, then the bellow of rage and fear he had been holding back.

She rang John at Betty's Caff. He came at once, by himself, as she had asked.

He heard the story, and went up to Ben in his room. Harriet stood outside the door, listening.

"You don't know your own strength, Hobbit, that's the trouble. It's wrong to hurt people."

"Are you angry with Ben? Are you going to hurt Ben?"

"Who's angry?" said John. "But if you hurt people, then they hurt you."

"Is Mary Jones going to hurt me?"

A silence. John was nonplussed.

"Take me to the caff with you? Take me now, take me away now."

She heard John looking for a clean pair of dungarees, heard him persuading Ben into them. She went down into the kitchen. John came down the stairs with Ben, who clung to his hand. John gave her a wink and a thumbs-up sign. He departed with Ben on his motorbike. She went to bring Paul home.

When she asked Dr. Brett to arrange an appointment with a specialist, she said, "Please don't make me out as some kind of hysterical idiot."

She took Ben to London. She left him in the care of Dr. Gilly's nurse. This doctor liked to see a child first, without its parents. It seemed sensible. Perhaps she is sensible, this one, thought Harriet, sitting by herself drinking coffee in a little café, and then wondered, What do I mean by that? What am I hoping for, this time? What she wanted, she decided, was that *at last* someone would use the right words, share the burden. No, she did not expect to be rescued, or even that anything much could change. She wanted to be acknowledged, her predicament given its value.

Well, was it likely? In conflict, half full of a longing for support, half cynical—*Well, what do you expect!*—she returned to find Ben with the nurse in a little room off the waiting-room. With his back to the wall, Ben watched the nurse's every movement, as a wary animal does. When he saw his mother, he rushed to her and hid behind her.

"Well," said the nurse tartly, "there's no need for *that*, Ben."

Harriet told Ben to sit down and wait for her: she was coming back soon. He got behind a chair and stood alert, his eyes on the nurse.

Then Harriet was sitting opposite a shrewd professional woman who had been told—Harriet was convinced—that this was an unreasonable worrying mother who couldn't handle her fifth child.

Dr. Gilly said, "I'm going to come straight to the point, Mrs. Lovatt. The problem is not with Ben, but with you. You don't like him very much."

"Oh my *God*," exploded Harriet, "not again!" She sounded peevish, whiny. She watched Dr. Gilly noting her reaction. "Dr. Brett told you that," she said. "Now you are saying it."

"Well, Mrs. Lovatt, would you say it is untrue? First I must say it is not your fault. And then that it is not uncommon. We can't choose what will turn up in the lottery—and that is what having a baby is. Luckily or unluckily, we can't choose. The first thing you have to do is not to blame yourself."

"I don't blame myself," said Harriet. "Though I don't expect you to believe it. But it's a bad joke. I feel I've been blamed for Ben ever since he was born. I feel like a criminal. I've always been made to feel like a criminal." During this complaint— shrill, but Harriet could not change her voice—years of bitterness came pouring out. Meanwhile Dr. Gilly sat looking at her desk. "It really is extraordinary! No one has ever said to me, no one, ever, 'How clever of you to have four marvellous normal clever good-looking children! They are a credit to you. Well done, Harriet!' Don't you think it is strange that no one has ever said it? But about Ben—I'm a criminal!"

Dr. Gilly enquired, after a pause for analysis of what Harriet had said, "You resent the fact that Ben isn't clever, is that it?"

"Oh my *God*," said Harriet violently. "What *is* the point!"

The two women eyed each other. Harriet sighed, letting her violence subside; the doctor was angry, but not showing it.

"Tell me," said Harriet, "are you saying that Ben is a perfectly normal child in every way? There's nothing strange about him?"

"He is within the range of normality. He is not very good at school, I am told, but often slow children catch up later."

"I can't believe it," said Harriet. "Look, just do something— oh all right, humour me! Ask the nurse to bring Ben in here."

Dr. Gilly considered this, then spoke into her machine.

They heard Ben shouting "No, no!" and the nurse's persuasive voice.

The door opened. Ben appeared: he had been pushed into the room by the nurse. The door shut behind him, and he backed against it, glaring at the doctor.

He stood with his shoulders hunched forward and his knees

bent, as if about to spring off somewhere. He was a squat, burly little figure, with a big head, the yellow stubble of his coarse hair growing from the double crown of his head into the point low on his heavy narrow forehead. He had a flattish flaring nose that turned up. His mouth was fleshy and curly. His eyes were like lumps of dull stone. For the first time Harriet thought, But he doesn't look like a six-year-old, but much older. You could almost take him for a little man, not a child at all.

The doctor looked at Ben. Harriet watched them both. The doctor then said, "All right, Ben, go out again. Your mother will be with you in a minute."

Ben stood petrified. Again Dr. Gilly spoke into her machine, the door opened, and Ben was hauled backwards out of sight, snarling.

"Tell me, Dr. Gilly, what did you see?"

Dr. Gilly's pose was wary, offended; she was calculating the time left to the end of the interview. She did not answer.

Harriet said, knowing it was no use, but because she wanted it said, heard: "He's not human, is he?"

Dr. Gilly suddenly, unexpectedly, allowed what she was thinking to express itself. She sat up, sighed heavily, put her hands to her face and drew them down, until she sat with her eyes shut, her fingers on her lips. She was a handsome middle-aged woman, in full command of her life, but for the flash of a moment an unlicensed and illegitimate distress showed itself, and she looked beside herself, even tipsy.

Then she decided to repudiate what Harriet knew was a moment of truth. She let her hands fall, smiled, and said jokingly, "From another planet? Outer space?"

"No. Well, you *saw* him, didn't you? How do we know what kinds of people—races, I mean—creatures different from us, have lived on this planet? In the past, you know? We don't really know, do we? How do we know that dwarves or goblins or hobgoblins, that kind of thing, didn't really live here? And that's why we tell stories about them? They really existed, once. . . . Well, how do we know they didn't?"

"You think Ben is a throwback?" enquired Dr. Gilly gravely. She sounded as if quite prepared to entertain the idea.

"It seems to me obvious," said Harriet.

Another silence, and Dr. Gilly examined her well-kept hands. She sighed. Then she looked up and met Harriet's eyes with "If that is so, then what do you expect me to do about it?"

Harriet insisted, "I want it *said*. I want it recognised. I just can't stand it never being said."

"Can't you see that it is simply outside my competence? If it is true, that is? Do you want me to give you a letter to the zoo, 'Put this child in a cage'? Or hand him over to science?"

"Oh God," said Harriet. "No, of course not."

Silence.

"Thank you, Dr. Gilly," said Harriet, ending the interview in the regular way. She stood up. "Would you be prepared to give me a prescription for a really strong sedative? There are times when I can't control Ben, and I have to have something to help me."

The doctor wrote. Harriet took the bit of paper. She thanked Dr. Gilly. She said goodbye. She went to the door, and glanced back. On the doctor's face she saw what she expected: a dark fixed stare that reflected what the woman was feeling, which was horror at the alien, rejection by the normal for what was outside the human limit. Horror of Harriet, who had given birth to Ben.

She found Ben alone in the little room, backed into a corner, glaring, unblinking, at the door she came in by. He was trembling. People in white uniforms, white coats, in rooms that smelled of chemicals . . . Harriet realised that without meaning it, she had reinforced her threats: If you behave badly, then . . .

He was subdued. He kept close to her; no, not like a child with its mother, but like a frightened dog.

Every morning now, she gave Ben a dose of the sedative, which, however, did not have much effect on him. But she hoped it would keep him damped down until school ended and he could roar off with John on the motorbike.

Then it was the end of Ben's first year at school. This meant that they could all go on, pretending that not much was wrong, he was just a "difficult" child. He wasn't learning anything, but then plenty of children did not: they put in time at school, and that was all.

That Christmas, Luke wrote to say he wanted to go to his grandparents, who were somewhere off the coast of southern Spain; and Helen went to Grandmother Molly's house in Oxford.

Dorothy came for Christmas, just three days. She took Jane back with her: Jane adored the little mongol child Amy.

Ben spent all his time with John. Harriet and David—when he was there, but he worked more and more—were with Paul through the Christmas holidays. Paul was even more difficult than Ben. But he was a normal "disturbed" child, not an alien.

Paul spent hours watching television. He escaped into it, watching restlessly, moving about as he watched, and ate, and ate—but never put on weight. Inside him seemed to be an unappeasable mouth that said, Feed me, feed me. He craved, every bit of him—for what? His mother's arms did not satisfy him, he was too restless to stay in them. He liked being with David, but never for long. It was the television that quieted him. Wars and riots; killings and hijackings; murders and thefts and kidnappings . . . the eighties, the barbarous eighties were getting into their stride and Paul lay sprawled in front of the set, or wandered about the room, eating and watching—being nourished. So it seemed.

The patterns for the family had been set: and so the future would be.

Luke always went for his school holidays to Grandfather James, with whom he "got on" so well. He liked his Grandmother Jessica, who was great fun, he said. His Aunt Deborah was fun, too: her attempts and failures at matrimony were a long-running serial story, presented comically. Luke was living with the rich, and thriving; and sometimes James brought him home to visit his parents, for the kindly man was unhappy at what went on in that misfortuned house, and knew that Harriet and David yearned for their eldest. They did visit him at his school for Sports Days; and Luke sometimes came home for half-terms.

Helen was happy at Molly's house. She lived in the room her father had once made his real home. She was old Frederick's favourite. She, too, sometimes came for a half-term.

Jane had prevailed on Dorothy to come and reason with Harriet and David, for she wanted to live with Dorothy and Aunt Sarah and the three healthy cousins and poor Amy. And so she did. Dorothy brought Jane home sometimes, and the parents could see that Dorothy had "talked" to Jane to make her kind to them, and never, not ever, criticise Ben.

Paul remained at home: he was there much more than Ben.

David said to Harriet, "What are we going to do with Paul?"

"What can we do?"

"He needs treatment of some kind. A psychiatrist . . ."

"What good is that going to do!"

"He's not learning anything, he's a real mess. He's worse than Ben! At least Ben is what he is, whatever that may be, and I don't think I want to know. But Paul . . ."

"And how are we going to pay for it?"

"I will."

David now added a part-time job teaching at a polytechnic to his already heavy load of work, and was hardly ever at home.

If he did come home during the week, it was late at night, and he fell into bed and slept, exhausted.

Paul was sent to "talk to someone," as the phrase goes.

He went nearly every afternoon after school. This was a success. The psychiatrist was a man of forty, with a family and a pleasant house. Paul stayed there for supper, and even went over to play with the children when he did not actually have an appointment to talk with the doctor.

Sometimes Harriet was alone in that great house all day, until Paul came home at about seven to watch the television—and Ben, too, though his television-watching was different. His attention was held by the screen unpredictably, and according to no pattern Harriet could see, usually only for a minute or two.

The two boys hated each other.

Once, Harriet found Paul in a corner of the kitchen, stretched up on tiptoes, trying to evade Ben's hands, which were reaching up to his throat. Short powerful Ben; tall spidery Paul—if Ben wanted to, he could kill Paul. Harriet thought that Ben was trying to frighten Paul, but Paul was hysterical. Ben grinned vindictively, full of triumph.

"Ben," said Harriet. "Ben—*down*." As if to a dog, warning it. "*Down*, Ben, *down*."

He turned sharply, saw her, dropped his hands. She put into her eyes the threat she had already used, her power over him: his memories of the past.

He bared his teeth and snarled.

Paul screamed, his terror bursting out of him. He raced up the stairs, slipping and falling, to get away from the horror that was Ben.

"If you ever do that again . . ." threatened Harriet. Ben went slowly to the big table and sat down. He was thinking, so she believed. "*If you ever do that again, Ben . . .*" He raised his eyes and looked at her. He was calculating, she could see. But what? Those cold, inhuman eyes . . . What did he see? People assumed he saw what they did, that he saw a human world. But perhaps his senses accommodated quite different facts, data. How could anyone know? What was he thinking? How did he see himself?

"Poor Ben," he would sometimes still say.

Harriet did not tell David about this incident. She knew he was at the edge of what he could stand. And what was she going to say? "Ben tried to kill Paul today!" This was a long way beyond what they had set for themselves, outside the permissible. Besides, she did not believe Ben was trying to kill Paul: he was demonstrating what he could do if he wanted to.

She told Paul that Ben was absolutely not trying to hurt him, only to frighten him. She thought Paul believed her.

Two years before Ben was due to leave the school where he learned nothing, but at least had not harmed anyone, John came to say he was departing from their lives. He had been granted a place in a job-training scheme in Manchester. He, and three of his mates.

Ben was there, listening. He had been told by John already, in Betty's Caff. But he had not taken it in. John had come up on purpose to say this to Harriet, with Ben present, so that Ben could accept it.

"Why can't I come, too?" demanded Ben.

"Because you can't, mate. But when I come and visit my mother and father, I'll come and see you."

Ben insisted, "But why can't I come with you?"

"Because I'll be at school, too. Not here. I'll be far away. Far, far away."

Ben stiffened. He assumed his rigid crouching pose, fists held out. He ground his teeth together, his eyes malevolent.

"Ben," said Harriet, using her special voice. "Ben, stop it."

"Come on now, Hobbit," said John, uneasy but kind. "I can't help it. I've got to get away from home some time, haven't I?"

"Is Barry going? Is Rowland going? Is Henry?"

"Yes, all four of us."

Suddenly, Ben rushed out into the garden, where he began kicking at a tree trunk, letting out squeals of rage.

"Better the tree than me," said John.

"Or me," said Harriet.

"I'm sorry," said John. "But there it is."

"I cannot imagine what we would have done without you," said Harriet.

He nodded, knowing it was true. And so John left their lives, for good. Ben had been with him almost every day of his life since he was rescued from the Institution.

Ben took it hard. At first, he did not believe it. When Harriet arrived to fetch him and, sometimes, Paul from school, he would be at the school gates, staring down the road where John had appeared gloriously on his motorbike. Reluctantly he went home with her, sitting in the corner of the back seat opposite from Paul, if Paul was not at the psychiatrist's, and his eyes searched the streets for signs of his lost friends. More than once, when he was not anywhere in the house, Harriet found him in Betty's Caff, sitting isolated at a table, his eyes on the door, where they might appear. In the street one morning, a minor member of John's gang was standing outside a shop-window, and Ben, crowing with pleasure, rushed to him: but the youth said casually, "Hi, it's Dumbo. Hello, Dopey," and turned away. Ben stood transfixed with disbelief, his mouth open, as if he had received a blow across it. It took him a long time to understand. As soon as he got home with Harriet and Paul, he would be off again, running into the centre of the town. She did not follow him. He would come back! He had nowhere else; and she was always pleased to have Paul alone with her—if Paul was there.

Once, Ben came thumping into the house, with his heavy run, and dived under the big table. A policewoman appeared and said to Harriet, "Where's that child? Is he all right?"

"He's under the table," said Harriet.

"Under the . . . but what for? I only wanted to make sure he wasn't lost. How old is he?"

"Older than he looks," said Harriet. "Come out, Ben, it's all right."

He would not come out: he was on all fours, facing where the policewoman stood, watching her neat shiny black shoes. He was remembering how once someone in a car had captured him and taken him away: uniforms, the aroma of officialdom.

"Well," said the policewoman. "Anyone'd think I was a child-snatcher! I shouldn't let him go running around like that. He might get himself kidnapped."

"No such luck," said Harriet, every inch the jolly coping mum. "More likely he'd kidnap them."

"It's like that, is it?"

And the policewoman departed, laughing.

David and Harriet lay side by side in their connubial bed, lights out, the house still. Two rooms down, Ben slept—they hoped. Four rooms down, at the end of the passage, Paul slept behind a self-locked door. It was late, and Harriet knew David would be asleep in a minute or two. They lay with a space between them. But it was no longer a space full of anger. Harriet knew that he was too permanently exhausted to be angry. Anyway, he had decided not to be angry: it was killing him. She always knew what he was thinking: he often answered, aloud, to her thoughts.

They sometimes made love, but she felt, and knew he did, that the ghosts of young Harriet and young David entwined and kissed.

It was as if the strain of her life had stripped off her a layer of flesh—not real flesh, but perhaps metaphysical substance, and invisible, unsuspected, until it had gone. And David, working as he did, had lost the self that was the family man. His efforts had made him successful in his firm, then gained him

112

a much better job in another. But that now was where his centre was: events have their own logic. He was now the sort of man he had once decided never to be. James no longer supported this family; he only paid for Luke. The candour, the openness that had come from David's stubborn trust in himself had been overlaid by his new self-confidence. Harriet knew that if she were to meet David now, for the first time, she would think him hard. But he was not hard. The rock she felt there in him was endurance. He knew how to stick things out. They were still alike.

Tomorrow, which was a Saturday, David was going to a cricket match at Luke's school. Harriet was visiting Helen at her school: Helen was in a play. Dorothy was coming in the morning to let the two escape for the weekend. Jane would not be with her, but at a party at a school friend's house she did not want to miss.

Paul was going with his father to visit his brother.

Ben would be alone with Dorothy, who had not seen him for a year.

Harriet was not surprised when David said, "Do you think Dorothy understands how much older Ben is than he looks?"

"Should we warn her?"

"But she understands everything, after about five minutes."

A silence. Harriet knew David was nearly asleep. He roused himself to say, "Harriet, has it occurred to you that in a couple of years' time Ben will be adolescent? He'll be a sexual being?"

"Yes, it has. But he's not on the same clock as we are."

"Presumably those people of his had something like an adolescence?"

"How do we know? Perhaps they weren't as sexual as we are. Someone said we're oversexed—who? Yes, it was Bernard Shaw."

"All the same, the thought of Ben sexual scares me."

"He hasn't hurt anyone for a long time."

After that weekend Dorothy said to Harriet, "I wonder if Ben ever asks himself why he is so different from us."

"How do we know? I've never known what he's thinking."

"Perhaps he thinks there's more of his kind somewhere."

"Perhaps he does."

"Provided it's not a female of the species!"

"Ben makes you think . . . all those different people who lived on the earth once—they must be in us somewhere."

"All ready to pop up! But perhaps we simply don't notice them when they do," said Dorothy.

"Because we don't want to," said Harriet.

"I certainly don't want to," said Dorothy. "Not after seeing Ben. . . . Harriet, do you and David realise that Ben isn't a child any longer? We treat him like one, but . . ."

Those two years before Ben could go to the big school were bad for him. He was lonely, but did he know he was? Harriet was very lonely, and knew she was. . . .

Like Paul, when he was there, Ben now went at once to the television when he came in from school. He sometimes watched from four in the afternoon until nine or ten at night. He did not seem to like one programme more than another. He did not understand that some programmes were for children, and others for grown-ups.

"What was the story of that film, Ben?"

"Story." He tried the word, his thick clumsy voice tentative. And his eyes were on her face, to discover what she wanted.

"What happened in that film, the one you've just seen?"

"Big cars," he would say. "A motorbike. That girl crying. Car chased the man."

Once, to see if Ben could learn from Paul, she said to Paul, "What was the story of that film?"

"It was about bank robbers, wasn't it?" said Paul, full of scorn for stupid Ben, who was listening, his eyes moving from his mother's face to his brother's. "They planned to rob the bank by tunnelling. They nearly reached the vault, but the police caught them in a trap. They went to prison, but most of them escaped. Two of them were shot by the police."

Ben had listened carefully.

"Tell me the story of the film, Ben?"

"Bank robbers," said Ben. And repeated what Paul had said, stumbling as he reached for exactly the same words.

"But that was only because I told him," said Paul.

Ben's eyes flared, but went cold as he told himself—Harriet presumed—"I mustn't hurt anyone. If I do, they'll take me to that place." Harriet knew everything Paul was thinking, feeling. But Ben—she had to try to guess.

Could Paul perhaps teach Ben, without either of them knowing it?

She would read a story to them both, and ask Paul to repeat the story. Then Ben copied Paul. But inside a few minutes he had forgotten it.

She played games like snakes-and-ladders and ludo with Paul, Ben watching; and then, when Paul was with his other family, she invited Ben to try. But he could not get the hang of the games.

Yet certain films he would watch over and over again and never tire of them. They had hired a video. He loved musicals: *The Sound of Music, West Side Story, Oklahoma!, Cats.*

"And now she is going to sing," Ben told her when she asked "What is happening now, Ben?"

Or, "They are going to dance around, and then she will sing." Or, "They are going to hurt that girl." "The girl ran away. Now it is a party."

But he could not tell her the story of the film.

"Sing me that tune, Ben. Sing it to me and Paul."

But he could not. He loved the tune, but could bring out only a rough, tuneless roar.

Harriet found Paul teasing Ben: asking him to sing a tune,

then taunting him. Harriet saw fury blaze in Ben's eyes, and told Paul not to do that ever again.

"Why *not?*" cried Paul. "Why not? It's always Ben, Ben, Ben . . ." He flailed his arms at Ben. Ben's eyes glittered. He was about to spring on Paul . . .

"*Ben,*" warned Harriet.

It seemed to her that these efforts she made to humanise him drove him away into himself, where he . . . but *what?*—remembered?—dreamed of?—his own kind.

Once, when she knew he was in the house, but could not find him, she went up from floor to floor looking into the rooms. The first floor, which was still inhabited, with David and herself, Ben and Paul, though three of the rooms were empty, their beds standing ready, spread with fresh pillows and laundered duvets. The second floor, with its clean empty rooms. The third floor: how long since children's voices, their laughter, filled that floor and spilled out of the open windows all over the garden? But Ben was not in any of those rooms. She went on quietly up to the attic. The door was open. From the high skylight fell a distorted rectangle of light, and in it stood Ben, staring up at dim sunlight. She could not make out what he wanted, what he felt. . . . He heard her and then she saw the Ben that this life he had to lead kept subdued: in one leap he had reached the dark at the edge of the eaves and vanished. All she could see was the obscurities of an attic that seemed boundless. She could hear nothing. He was crouching there, staring out at her. . . . She felt the hair on her head lift, felt cold chills—instinctive, for she did not fear him with her mind. She was rigid with terror.

"Ben," she said softly, though her voice shook. "Ben . . ." putting into the word her human claim on him, and on this wild dangerous attic where he had gone back into a far-away past that did not know human beings.

No reply. Nothing. A blotch of shadow momentarily dimmed

the thin dirty light under the skylight: a bird had passed, on its way from one tree to another.

She went downstairs, and sat cold and lonely in the kitchen, drinking hot tea.

Just before Ben went to the local secondary modern school, the only school of course that would have him, there was a summer holiday, almost like those in the past. People had written each other, had rung: "Those poor people, let's go there, at least for a week. . . ." Poor David . . . always that, Harriet knew. Sometimes, rarely, poor Harriet . . . More often, irresponsible Harriet, selfish Harriet, crazy Harriet . . .

Who had not let Ben be murdered, she defended herself fiercely, in thought, never aloud. By everything they—the society she belonged to—stood for, believed in, she had had no alternative but to bring Ben back from that place. But because she had, and saved him from murder, she had destroyed her family. Had harmed her life . . . David's . . . Luke's, Helen's, Jane's . . . and Paul's. Paul, the worst.

Her thoughts circled in this groove.

David kept saying she should simply not have gone up there . . . but how could she *not* have gone, being Harriet? And if she had not, she believed David would have.

A scapegoat. She was the scapegoat—Harriet, the destroyer of her family.

But another layer of thoughts, or feelings, ran deeper. She said to David, "We are being punished, that's all."

"What for?" he demanded, already on guard because there was a tone in her voice he hated.

"For presuming. For thinking we could be happy. Happy because *we* decided we would be."

"Rubbish," he said. Angry: this Harriet made him angry. "It was chance. Anyone could have got Ben. It was a chance gene, that's all."

"I don't think so," she stubbornly held on. "We were going

to be happy! No one else is, or I never seem to meet them, but we were going to be. And so down came the thunderbolt."

"Stop it, Harriet! Don't you know where that thought leads? Pogroms and punishments, witch-burnings and angry Gods—!" He was shouting at her.

"And scapegoats," said Harriet. "Don't forget the scapegoats."

"Vindictive Gods, from thousands of years ago," he hotly contended, disturbed to his depths, she could see. "Punishing Gods, distributing punishments for insubordination . . ."

"But who were *we* to decide we were going to be this or that?"

"Who? *We* did. Harriet and David. *We* took the responsibility for what we believed in, and we did it. Then—bad luck. That's all. We could easily have succeeded. We could have had just what we planned. Eight children in this house and everyone happy . . . Well, as far as possible."

"And who paid for it? James. And Dorothy, in a different way . . . No, I'm just stating facts, David, not criticising *you*."

But this had long ago ceased to be a sore point with David. He said: "James and Jessica have so much money they wouldn't have missed three times as much. Anyway, they adored doing it. And Dorothy—she complained about being used, but she's been Amy's nursemaid ever since she got fed up with us."

"We just wanted to be better than everyone else, that's all. We thought we were."

"No, that's how you are twisting it around now. All we wanted was—to be ourselves."

"Oh, that's all," said Harriet airily, spitefully. "That's all."

"Yes. Don't do it, Harriet, stop it. . . . Well, if you won't, if you have to, then leave me out. I'm not going to be dragged back to the Middle Ages."

"Is that where we've been dragged back to?"

Molly and Frederick came, bringing Helen. They had not, would not, forgive Harriet, but Helen must be considered. She was doing well at school, an attractive, self-sufficient girl of sixteen. But cool, distant.

James brought Luke, eighteen years old, a handsome boy, quiet, reliable and steady. He was going to build boats, like his grandfather. He was a watcher, an observer, like his father.

Dorothy came with Jane, fourteen. Non-academic, but "none the worse for that," as Dorothy insisted. "I could never pass an exam." The "and look at me" was unspoken; but Dorothy would challenge them all simply by her presence. Which was less substantial than it had been. She was rather thin these days, and sat about a good deal. Paul, eleven years old, was histrionic, hysterical, always demanding attention. He talked a lot about his new school, a day-school, which he hated. He wanted to know why he couldn't go to boarding-school like all the others. David said, forestalling James with a proud look, that he would pay for it.

"Surely it is time you sold this house," Molly said, and what she was saying to her selfish daughter-in-law was "And then my son can stop killing himself working too hard for you."

David came in quickly to support Harriet, "I agree with Harriet, we shouldn't sell the house yet."

"Well, what do you think is going to change?" asked Molly, cold. "Ben certainly isn't."

But privately David said something else. He would like the house sold.

"It's being with Ben in a small house, just the thought of it," said Harriet.

"It wouldn't have to be a small house. But does it have to be the size of a hotel?"

David knew that even now, though it was foolish, she could not finally give up her dreams of the old life coming back.

Then that holiday was gone. A success, on the whole, for everyone tried hard. Except for Molly—so Harriet saw it. But it was sad for both parents. They had to sit listening to talk about people they had not met, only heard of. Luke and Helen visited families of school friends. And these people could never be asked here.

In September of the year Ben became eleven, he went to the big school. It was 1986.

Harriet prepared herself for the telephone call that must come from the headmaster. It would be, she thought, towards the end of the first term. The new school would have been sent a report on Ben, from the headmistress who had so consistently refused to acknowledge that there was anything remarkable about him. "Ben Lovatt is not an academic child, but . . ." But what? "He tries hard." Would that have been it? But he had long ago stopped trying to understand what he was taught, could hardly read or write, more than his name. He still tried to fit in, to copy others.

There was no telephone call, no letter. Ben, whom she examined for bruises every evening when he came home, seemed to have entered the tough and often brutal world of the secondary school without difficulty.

"Do you like this school, Ben?"
"Yes."
"Better than the other school?"
"Yes."

As everyone knows, all these schools have a layer, like a sediment, of the uneducable, the unassimilable, the hopeless, who move up the school from class to class, waiting for the happy moment when they can leave. And, more often than not, they are truants, to the relief of their teachers. Ben had at once become one of these.

Some weeks after he went to the big school, he brought home a large, shaggy dark youth, full of easy good nature. Harriet thought, John! And then, But he must be John's brother! No;

Ben had been drawn to this boy, it was clear, first of all because of his memories of that happy time with John. But his name was Derek, and he was fifteen, soon to leave school. Why did he put up with Ben, years younger than he was? Harriet watched the two as they helped themselves to food from the refrigerator, made themselves tea, sat in front of the television, talking more than they watched. In fact, Ben seemed older than Derek. They ignored her. Just as when Ben was the mascot, the pet of the gang of youths, John's gang, and had seemed to see only John, now his attention was for Derek. And, soon, for Billy, for Elvis, and for Vic, who came in a gang after school and sat around and fed themselves from the refrigerator.

Why did these big boys like Ben?

She would look at them, from the stairs perhaps, as she came down into the living-room, a group of youths, large, or thin, or plump, dark, fair, or redheaded—and among them Ben, squat, powerful, heavy-shouldered, with his bristly yellow hair growing in that strange pattern, with his watchful, alien eyes— and she thought, But he's not really younger than they are! He's much shorter, yes. But it almost seems that he dominates them. When they sat around the big family table, talking in their style, which was loud, raucous, jeering, jokey, they were always look- ing at Ben. Yet he spoke very little. When he did say something, it was never much more than Yes, or No. Take this! Get that! Give me—whatever it was, a sandwich, a bottle of Coke. And he watched them carefully all the time. He was the boss of this gang, whether they knew it or not.

They were a bunch of gangly, spotty, uncertain adolescents; he was a young adult. She had to conclude this finally, though for a while she believed that these poor children, who stayed together because they were found stupid, awkward, and unable to match up to their contemporaries, liked Ben because he was even clumsier and more inarticulate than they. No! She dis-

covered that "Ben Lovatt's gang" was the most envied in the
school, and a lot of boys, not only the truants and drop-outs,
wanted to be part of it.

Harriet watched Ben with his followers and tried to imagine
him among a group of his own kind, squatting in the mouth
of a cave around roaring flames. Or a settlement of huts in a
thick forest? No, Ben's people were at home under the earth,
she was sure, deep underground in black caverns lit by torches—
that was more like it. Probably those peculiar eyes of his were
adapted for quite different conditions of light.

She often sat in the kitchen, by herself, when they were across
the low wall in the living-room, watching the box. They might
sprawl there for hours, all afternoon and evening. They made
tea, raided the refrigerator, went out to fetch pies, or chips, or
pizzas. They did not seem to mind what they watched; they
liked the afternoon soap operas, did not turn off the children's
programmes; but best of all they enjoyed the bloody fare of the
evening. Shootings and killings and tortures and fighting: this
is what fed them. She watched them watching—but it was more
as if they were actually part of the stories on the screen. They
were unconsciously tensing and flexing, faces grinning, or
triumphant or cruel; and they let out groans or sighs or yells of
excitement: "That's it, *do* it!" "Carve him up!" "Kill him, slice
him!" And the moans of excited participation as the bullets
poured into a body, as blood spurted, as the tortured victim
screamed.

These days the local newspapers were full of news of mug-
gings, hold-ups, break-ins. Sometimes this gang, Ben among
them, did not come into the Lovatts' house for a whole day,
two days, three.

"Where have you been, Ben?"

He replied indifferently, "Been with my friends."

"Yes, but where?"

"Been around."

In the park, in a café, in the cinema, and, when they could borrow (or steal?) motorbikes, off to some seaside town.

She thought of ringing the headmaster, but then: What is the point? If I were in his place, I'd be relieved they took themselves off.

The police? Ben in the hands of the police?

The gang always seemed to have plenty of money. More than once, dissatisfied with what they found in the refrigerator, they brought in feasts of food, and ate all evening. Derek (never Ben!) would offer her some.

"Like a bit of take-away, love?"

And she accepted, but sat apart from them, for she knew they would not want her too close.

There were rapes, too, among those news items. . . .

She examined those faces, trying to match them with what she had read. Ordinary young men's faces; they all seemed older than fifteen, sixteen. Derek had a foolish look to him: at ugly moments on the screen he laughed a lot in a weak excitable way. Elvis was a lean, sharp blond youth, very polite, but a nasty customer, she thought, with eyes as cold as Ben's. Billy was a hulk, stupid, with aggression in every movement. He would get so lost in the violence on the box that he would jump to his feet and seem almost to disappear into the screen—and then the others jeered at him, and he came to himself and sat down. He scared her. They all did. But, she thought, they weren't all that intelligent. Perhaps Elvis was. . . . If they were stealing (or worse), then who planned it all, and looked after them?

Ben? "He does not know his own strength." That formula had gone with him through school. How did he control the rages that she knew could overcome him? She was always co-vertly on the watch for cuts, bruises, wounds. All had them, but nothing very bad.

One morning, she came down the stairs to find Ben eating

breakfast with Derek. That time she said nothing, but knew she could expect more. Soon she found six of them at breakfast: she had heard them, very late, creep upstairs and find beds for themselves.

She stood by the table, looked at them bravely, ready to face them out, and said, "You aren't just to sleep here, any time you feel like it." They kept their heads down and went on eating.

"I mean it," she insisted.

Derek said, laughing, intending to sound insolent, "Oh, sorry, sorry, sorry I'm *sure*. But we thought you wouldn't mind."

"I do mind," she said.

"It's a big house," said Billy the lout, the one she was most afraid of. He did not look at her, but crammed food into his mouth, and made a noise eating.

"It's not your house," said Harriet.

"One day we'll take it away from you," said Elvis, laughing loudly.

"Oh, perhaps you will, yes."

They all made "revolutionary" remarks like this, when they remembered.

"Come the revolution, we'll . . . " "We'll kill all the rich shits and then . . . " "There's one law for the rich, and one for the poor, everybody knows *that*." They would say these things amiably, with that air of repletion people use when copying what others do; when they are part of a popular mood or movement.

David came back from work late, these days, and sometimes did not come at all. He stayed with one of the people he worked with. It happened that he arrived early one night and found the gang, nine or ten of them, watching television, with beer cans, cartons of take-away Chinese, papers that had held fish and chips, all over the floor.

He said, "Clear that mess up."

They slowly got to their feet and cleared it up. He was a man: the man of the house. Ben cleared up with them.

"That's enough," said David. "And now go home, all of you."

They trailed off, and Ben went with them. Neither Harriet nor David said anything to stop him.

They had not been alone together for some time. Weeks, she thought. He wanted to say something, but was afraid to—afraid of arousing that dangerous anger of his?

"Can't you see what is going to happen?" he finally asked, sitting down with a plate of whatever he could find in the refrigerator.

"You mean, they are going to be here more often?"

"Yes, that's what I mean. Can't you see we should sell this place?"

"Yes, I know we should," she said quietly, but he mistook her tone.

"For God's sake, Harriet, what can you be waiting for? It's crazy. . . ."

"The only thing I can think of now is that the children might be pleased we kept it."

"We have no children, Harriet. Or, rather, I have no children. *You* have one child."

She felt that he would not be saying this if he were here more often. She said, "There is something you aren't seeing, David."

"And what's that?"

"Ben will leave. They'll all be off, and Ben will go with them."

He considered this; considered her, his jaws moving slowly as he ate. He looked very tired. He was also looking much older than he was, could easily be taken as sixty, rather than fifty. He was a grey, rather stooped, shadowy man, with a strained look, and a wary glance that expected trouble. This was what he was directing at her now.

"Why? They can come here any time they like, do what they like, help themselves to food."

"It's not exciting enough for them, that's why. I think they'll just drift off one day to London, or some big town. They went off for five days last week."

"And Ben will go with them?"

"Ben will go with them."

"And you won't go after him and bring him back?"

She did not reply. This was unfair, and he must know it; after a moment or two, he said, "Sorry. I'm so tired I don't know whether I'm coming or going."

"When he's gone, perhaps we could go and have a holiday together somewhere."

"Well, perhaps we could." This sounded as if he might even believe it, hope for it.

Later they lay side by side, not touching, and talked practically about arrangements for visiting Jane at her school. And there was Paul, at his, with a Parents' Visiting Day.

They were alone in the big room where all the children but Ben had been born. Above them the emptiness of the upper floors, and the attic. Downstairs, the empty living-room and kitchen. They had locked the doors. If Ben decided to come home that night, he would have to ring.

She said, "With Ben gone, we could sell this and buy some sensible house somewhere. Perhaps the children would enjoy coming to visit if he wasn't there."

No reply: David was asleep.

Soon after that, Ben and the others went off again for some days. She saw them on the television. There was a riot in North London. "Trouble" had been forecast. They were not among those throwing bricks, lumps of iron, stones, but stood in a group at one side, leering and jeering and shouting encouragement.

Next day they returned, but did not settle down to watching

television. They were restless, and went off again. Next morning the news was that a small shop had been broken into, one that had a post-office counter in it. About four hundred pounds had been taken. The shopkeeper had been bound and gagged. The postmistress was beaten up and left unconscious.

At about seven that night they came in. Except for Ben, they were full of excitement and achievement. When they saw her, they exchanged glances, enjoying the secret she did not share. She saw them pull out wads of notes, fingering them, pushing them back into pockets. If she were the police, she would be suspicious on the strength of their elation, their hectic faces.

Ben was not fevered, like the others. He was as he always was. You could think he had not been part of—whatever it was. But he had been there at the riot, she had seen him.

She tried: "I saw you lot on the television, you were at the Whitestone Estates."

"Oh yeah, we were there," boasted Billy.

"That was us," said Derek, giving himself thumbs-up approval, and Elvis looked sharp and knowing. Some others with them, who came sometimes, not regulars, looked pleased.

A few days later, she remarked, "I think you lot ought to know that this house is going to be sold—not at once, but quite soon."

She was watching Ben particularly, but while he did turn his eyes on her, and—she supposed—took the news in, he said nothing.

"So you're going to sell, then?" said Derek, she felt as much for politeness as for anything.

She waited for Ben to mention it, but he did not. Was his identification with this gang of his now so great that he did not think of this as his home?

She remarked to him, when he was out of earshot of the others, "Ben, if for some reason you can't find me here, I'm going to give you an address where you can always reach me."

As she spoke, she felt that David was watching her satirically, disapprovingly. "All right," she said silently to the invisible David, "but I know you would do the same, if I didn't. . . . That is the kind of person we are, and there's nothing we can do about it, for better or worse."

Ben took the sheet of paper on which she had written her name, Harriet Lovatt, care of Molly and Frederick Burke and their Oxford address, which did give her a certain spiteful pleasure. But she found the sheet of paper lying forgotten or unregarded on the floor of his room, and did not try again.

It was spring, then summer, and they came less often, sometimes not for days at a time. Derek had acquired a motorbike.

Now, whenever she heard of a break-in, or a mugging, or a rape anywhere, she blamed them; but thought she was unjust. They could not be blamed for everything! Meanwhile, she was longing for them to leave. She was a ferment of need to start a new life. She wanted to be done with this unhappy house, and the thoughts that went with it.

But they did come, sometimes. As if they had not been absent for so long, saying nothing about where, they would drift into the living-room, and sit themselves around the set, four or five of them, sometimes as many as ten or eleven. They did not now raid the refrigerator: there was very little in it these days. They brought in enormous quantities of a variety of foodstuffs that originated in a dozen countries. Pizzas, and quiches; Chinese food, and Indian; pita bread filled with salad; tacos, tortillas, samosas, chili con carne; pies and pasties and sandwiches. These were the conventional and hidebound English, were they? Not prepared to eat anything but what their parents knew! It did not seem to matter to them what they ate, provided there was a lot of it, and they might strew crumbs and crusts and cartons about, and not have to clean anything up.

She tidied up after them and thought: It's not for long.

She would sit by herself at the big table while they sprawled about on the other side of the low wall, and the television noises made a counter-current to their loud, noisy, rancorous voices—the voices of an alienated, non-comprehending, hostile tribe.

The expanse of the table soothed her. When first bought, as a discarded butcher's table, it had had a rough, much-cut-about surface, but it had been planed down, and at that stage of its life had shown the clean creamy white of the new layer of wood. She and David had waxed it. Since then, thousands of hands, fingers, sleeves, the bare forearms of summer, the cheeks of children who had fallen forward asleep sitting on adults' laps, the plump feet of toddlers held up to walk there, everyone applauding: all this, the smoothings and caressings of twenty years, had given the wide board—it was all of a piece, cut long ago from some gigantic oak—a gleaming silken surface, so smooth fingers skated over it. Beneath this skin the knots and whorls lay submerged, their pattern known intimately to her. The skin had been scarred, though. Here was a brown half-circle where Dorothy had set down a too hot saucepan and, angry with herself, had snatched it up. There was a curving black weal, but Harriet could not remember what had made it. If you looked at the table from a certain angle, it had areas of tiny dimples or dents, where trivets had been set to keep the heat of dishes off the precious surface.

When she leaned forward, she could see herself in the gleam—dully, but enough to make her lean back again, out of sight. She looked like David: old. No one would say she was forty-five. But it was not the ordinary ageing of grey hair, tired skin: invisible substance had been leached from her; she had been drained of some ingredient that everyone took for granted, which was like a layer of fat but was not material.

Leaning back where she could not see her blurry image, she imagined how, once, this table had been set for feasts and enjoyment, for—family life. She re-created the scenes of twenty, fifteen, twelve, ten years ago, the stages of the Lovatt board, first David and herself, brave innocents, with his parents, and Dorothy, and her sisters . . . then the babies appearing, and becoming small children . . . new babies . . . twenty people, thirty, had crowded around this gleaming surface and been mirrored in it, they had added other tables to the ends, broadened it with planks set on trestles . . . she saw the table lengthen, and widen, and the faces mass around it, always smiling faces, for this dream could not accommodate criticism or discord. And the babies . . . the children . . . she heard the laughter of small children, their voices; and then the wide shine of the table seemed to darken, and there was Ben, the alien, the destroyer. She turned her head cautiously, afraid to alert in him senses she was sure he possessed, and saw him there, in his chair. He sat apart from the others, always apart; and, as always, his eyes were on others' faces, observing. Cold eyes? She had always thought them cold; but what did they see? Thoughtful? One could believe him thinking, taking in data from what he saw and arranging it—but according to inner patterns neither she nor anyone else could guess at. Compared with the raw and unfinished youths, he was a mature being. Finished. Complete. She felt she was looking, through him, at a race that reached its apex thousands and thousands of years before humanity, whatever that meant, took this stage. Did Ben's people live in caves underground while the ice age ground overhead, eating fish from dark subterranean rivers, or sneaking up into the bitter snow to snare a bear, or a bird—or even people, her (Harriet's) ancestors? Did his people rape the females of humanity's fore-bears? Thus making new races, which had flourished and de-parted, but perhaps had left their seeds in the human matrix, here and there, to appear again, as Ben had? (And perhaps Ben's genes were already in some foetus struggling to be born?)

Did he feel her eyes on him, as a human would? He some-times looked at her while she looked at him—not often, but it did happen that his eyes met hers. She would put into her gaze these speculations, these queries, her need, her *passion* to know more about him—whom, after all, she had given birth to, had carried for eight months, though it had nearly killed her—but he did not feel the questions she was asking. Indifferently, casually, he looked away again, and his eyes went to the faces of his mates, his followers.

And saw—what?

Did he ever remember now that she—his mother, but what did that mean to him?—had found him in that place, and brought him home? Had found him a poor creature half dead in a strait-jacket? Did he know that because she had brought him home, this house had emptied itself, and everyone had gone away, leaving her alone?

Around and around and around: if I had let him die, then all of us, so many people, would have been happy, but I could not do it, and therefore . . .

And what would happen to Ben now? He already knew about the half-derelict buildings, the caves and caverns and shelters of the big cities where people lived who could not find a place in ordinary homes and houses: he must do, for where else could he have been during the periods of days, or weeks, when he was gone from home? Soon, if he was often enough part of great crowds, part of the element looking for excitement in riots, street fights, he and his friends would be known to the police. He was not someone easily overlooked . . . yet why did she say that? Everyone in authority had *not* been seeing Ben ever since he was born. . . . When she saw him on television in that crowd, he had worn a jacket with its collar up, and a scarf, and was like a younger brother, perhaps of Derek. He seemed a stout schoolboy. Had he put on those clothes to disguise himself? Did that mean that he knew how he looked? How did he see himself?

Would people always refuse to see him, to recognise what he was?

It would not, could not, be someone in authority, who would then have to take responsibility. No schoolteacher, or doctor, or specialist had been able to say, "That is what he is": neither could any policeman, or police doctor, or social worker. But suppose one day someone who was an amateur of the human condition, perhaps an anthropologist of an unusual kind, actually saw Ben, let's say standing on a street with his mates, or in a police court, and admitted the truth. Admitted curiosity . . . what then? Could Ben, even now, end up sacrificed to science? What would they do with him? Carve him up? Examine those cudgel-like bones of his, those eyes, and find out why his speech was so thick and awkward?

If this did not happen—and her experience with him until now said it was unlikely—then what she foresaw for him was even worse. The gang would continue to support themselves by theft, and sooner or later would be caught. Ben, too. In police hands he would fight, and roar and stamp about and bellow, out of control with rage, and they would drug him, because they had to, and before very long he would be as he had been when she had found him dying, looking like a giant slug, pallid and limp in his cloth shroud.

Or perhaps he could evade being caught? Was he clever enough? These mates of his, his gang, certainly were not, giving themselves away by their excitement, their elation.

Harriet sat on there quietly, with the television sounds and their voices coming from next door; and she sometimes looked at Ben quickly, and then away; and she wondered how soon they would all simply go off, perhaps not knowing they would not return. She would sit there, beside the quiet soft shine of the pool that was the table, and wait for them to come back, but they would not come back.

And why should they stay in this country? They could easily take off and disappear into any number of the world's great cities, join the underworld there, live off their wits. Perhaps quite soon, in the new house she would be living in (alone) with David, she would be looking at the box, and there, in a shot on the News of Berlin, Madrid, Los Angeles, Buenos Aires, she would see Ben, standing rather apart from the crowd, staring at the camera with his goblin eyes, or searching the faces in the crowd for another of his own kind.

A NOTE ON THE TYPE

The text of this book was set in a digitized version of
Electra, a typeface designed by W. A. Dwiggins (1880–
1956). This face cannot be classified as either modern or
old style. It is not based on any historical model; nor does
it echo any particular period or style. It avoids the extreme
contrasts between thick and thin elements that mark most
modern faces and attempts to give a feeling of fluidity,
power, and speed.

Composed by
PennSet, Inc. Bloomsburg, Pennsylvania

Printed and bound by
Fairfield Graphics, Fairfield, Pennsylvania

Typography and binding design
by Dorothy Schmiderer